THE LOST BIRD

A THRILLER BY

J.K. KELLY

Library of Congress Control Number: Pending

ISBN: *979-8-9891416-3-0* paperback

ISBN: *979-8-9891416-4-7* eBook

Cover photography provided by Jim Raeder.

The Lost Bird
is dedicated to the brave pilots and crews of
the Warbirds of World War II
and to the men, women, events, and
museums who continue to honor them.

Special thanks to
Chris Polhemus and Jodi Beyer,
who helped make this all possible.

CHAPTER ONE

Schiphol Airport, Amsterdam

THE INTENTIONAL FOUR-HOUR layover in Istanbul had provided retired Marine Chris Boone from Texas with enough time to taxi to a spot near the Blue Mosque, where he rendezvoused with another operator for the CIA. Over strong coffee, they caught up about their time in the Marines. More importantly, at least for the CIA, was the download and debrief he shared of everything he had been working on before taking a reluctant but necessary break from the action and adrenaline he craved. At Schiphol, Chris found himself admiring an array of fresh tulips on display at a flower stand across from a Starbucks. The flower's scent made him smile as he held the single potted purple tulip to his nose. He laughed as he noticed his manicured nails, a bit of indulgence he'd gone for on his last day in the Gulf. As far as his friends and family back home knew, he worked offshore oil rigs all over the globe. When anyone commented on a lack of grease under his nails or callouses on his hands, he falsely reminded them that he operated drones that inspected the rigs. "They don't get very dirty working a few joysticks," he'd always say with a laugh. As an elderly woman approached him from behind, she caught him off-guard.

"Your wife or girlfriend will love it," the woman said in a French accent. Chris turned to her and nodded.

"She's long gone," he told her. The woman's face showed disappointment.

"Perhaps your mother then," she suggested. Chris shook his head no.

"She's gone too," he said. Undeterred, the woman tried again.

"Then a sister?" she asked, an expression of hope forcing a half smile. Chris shook his head no again and grinned.

"She'd ask, what'd you do now?" Finally, the woman let out a faint laugh and patted Chris' arm. He smiled at her, stepped to the counter to pay, and then found the woman as she walked out of the store and scanned a bank of monitors for her gate. Stepping in front of her, her face showed confusion momentarily, but then she smiled as he handed her the flower.

"For you," he said, then walked across to his gate and joined the long line of passengers preparing to board the ten-hour flight to Houston.

∽

Palm Springs, California

FROM ITS VANTAGE point on the ground, the small brown desert hare went about his business on a beautiful Saturday morning as he sniffed for food. The sun's warmth took the chill off what lingered from a particularly cool night in early October. While watching for the shadows cast by his natural enemy, birds of prey, the hare suddenly froze as the ground beneath it vibrated. But this wasn't an earth-quake. It was something much different, man-made. Soon, another bird of prey would be upon it. Powered by its four 1200-horsepower engines, as the beautifully restored World War II B-17 bomber roared toward the end of the runway, the hare bolted for the nearest brush just as the plane's shadow darkened the ground around it. Seconds later, as the animal's heartbeat slowed, the passengers' hearts aboard a once-in-a-lifetime plane ride pounded in their chests. From the cockpit, as they quickly climbed to an altitude of 10,000 feet, veteran wartime and commercial pilot Pat Monaghan, a lanky, sunbaked seventy-year-old from Reno, Nevada, greeted the paying customers through the headsets they wore to muffle the roar.

"Welcome aboard one of the most famous warplanes ever made," Monaghan began. "This B-17 flying fortress and thousands like her defeated Hitler and Nazi Germany in the skies over Europe during the Second World War. Unfortunately, less than a handful of these incredible air-planes – another product of the greatest generation, are still flying today, and it is an honor and a privilege for me to be your pilot today." Thirty feet behind Monaghan and his co-pilot Charlie Taylor, a fifty-five-old retired C-130 pilot and warbird lover like Monaghan, four passengers had no idea their lives were in danger.

⤳

Benny Armstrong's son John had surprised his father with a very special present for the man's seventieth birthday – a seat on this warbird ride. The two men sat on a red canvas bench on the starboard side of the plane just a few feet from a once lethal but now disabled .50 caliber machine gun. John was busy taking photos and videos with his phone as Benny smiled at the young couple from San Diego seated directly across from them. They'd gotten to know one another while standing in line waiting to board; Walt and Christa were headed to Las Vegas afterward, eloping to one of the wedding chapels on the strip. Benny laughed as the woman's long blonde hair danced in the air from the waist gunner's window openings. He watched as Walt studied the ribbon of ammunition that fed the .50 caliber on his side of the plane. Suddenly, a man wearing aviators and dressed in black shoved his way between the four.

"Well, excuse me," the senior Armstrong shouted as he watched the man continue toward the front of the plane without looking back. He turned to his son.

"What an asshole," he shouted. John couldn't hear his father over the roar of the engines, but he read his father's lips and nodded in agreement. Not allowing the rude behavior to ruin another moment, the four returned their focus to the spectacular warplane they were aboard. Walt gestured to his fiancé who smiled as she lifted the left side of her headphones as he leaned in.

"My grandfather flew in one of these during the war," he yelled proudly. "He sat in this position while the flak and the Luftwaffe shot the shit out of his plane run after run." But then he grew quiet. Wells nodded and began to refocus on the ride, but Chapman needed to say more.

"My dad told me grandpa gave the enemy hell, though, and turned a lot of German planes into Swiss cheese before he died in one of these on the way back to their base in England." Wells' expression turned sorrowful as she let go of the headphones and touched his. Chapman smiled at her and wrapped his arm around her shoulder. Across from them, the Armstrongs were beaming.

"Think we'll see the Hoover Dam from up here?" John shouted to his father. Benny shook his head no and then leaned close to his son, shouting, "Can you imagine what it was like when they saw the English Channel for the first time?" John thought for a moment and then answered the question.

"Coming or going?" John yelled. "It's hard to comprehend how many never made it back alive." The men sat back in their seats, their faces revealing the enormity of all that had happened in planes just like this one to the airmen, many of whom were just teenagers. Then, an announcement from Pat Monaghan gave the passengers an update.

"We've reached our cruising altitude now, so as we said in our pre-flight briefing, you are free to walk about the plane, but remember, try and grab hold of something stationary as you move about just in case we find a few bumps in the air up here and remember, this is sacred ground so be sure to treat her with the utmost care and respect." Walt and Christa got up from their seats and headed back toward the tail gunner position while John and Benny gazed out the waist gunner's windows. Up front, the man who had brushed past them just a minute earlier approached the cockpit.

∽

He nodded at the two male passengers seated near the radioman's desk. They seemed harmless, in their seventies, one wearing a well-worn Vietnam Veteran's ball cap and the other a bright red Phillies cap. Then he moved across the catwalk that spanned the bomb bay doors. As he came close to the cockpit, he stopped for a moment. He looked back into the plane and was pleased nobody had followed him. That would have changed everything, at least for them. Then, he pulled a gun from inside his black jacket, racked the slide to chamber a bullet, and made his move.

✖

Pat Monaghan and Charlie Taylor loved what they were doing. Flying had been a lifelong passion for them both, had become their profession, and their careers and relationships had enabled them to do what so few could – be given the rare responsibility of flying a B17 and then bringing its passengers and crew home safely time and time again. Pat looked out his side cockpit window, scanned the controls and gauges, and then looked toward his friend seated to his right. Things were going as planned, but then he saw the barrel of a gun, a black Beretta 9mm, being pressed against the back of his head.

✖

The intruder wore black latex mehanic's gloves as he held the gun with his right hand and pressed the barrel harder into the co-pilot's neck as he removed a 3x5" index card from his jacket pocket and handed it to him. It read in bold black letters:

WE HAVE OTHERS ON THE PLANE.
NO SUDDEN MOVES OR SOMEONE GETS SHOT.
DO NOT RADIO OR SIGNAL ANYONE.

DO AS YOU ARE TOLD AND NOBODY GETS HURT.

NOD YOU UNDERSTAND.

The co-pilot nodded and then held the card out for Monahan to read. The gunman watched as the pilots stared at each other through their aviators. With no response from the pilot, the gunman suddenly moved the gun to the side of Monahan's head and poked at it. Without a reaction, he pushed the barrel in harder. After a second, he finally got a nod from the pilot, and Pat turned his head abruptly to shake free of the weapon. The gunman slid the first note into the back pocket of his black jeans, removed another from his jacket pocket, and handed the co-pilot a second card.

INFORM THE PASSENGERS ALL IS OK

BUT YOU NEED TO LAND TO CHECK OIL PRESSURE IN ONE OF THE ENGINES

HAPPENS ALL THE TIME. NOTHING TO WORRY ABOUT

TELL THEM TO RETURN TO THEIR SEATS AND BUCKLE UP

CHARLIE – WE HAVE SOMEONE WATCHING YOUR WIFE LINDA

DO AS YOU ARE TOLD, AND NOBODY WILL GET HURT.

The gunman watched as the co-pilot tensed when he read his wife's name on the card and leaned in close, raising the co-pilot's left headset, shouting, "She'll be okay. Just don't do anything stupid."

Charlie pulled his head away, the headset slapping back over his ear. The gunman watched and waited for Charlie to obey orders, and when he didn't, the gunman smacked the co-pilot on the side of the head with the gun. Suddenly, Pat began to move, reaching for the gun, but without flinching, the gunman shoved the barrel toward the pilot's face. The broken aviators fell into Pat's lap as the barrel stopped against the pilot's right temple. The gunman turned to Charlie and shouted, "Show him the card. Now!" As the co-pilot shook his head in apparent frustration and disbelief, he passed the card to Pat, who pulled back away from the gun barrel as he took the note and read it. He watched as the pilot and co-pilot stared into the blue sky surrounding them and then relented. He watched as Pat picked up his sunglasses, saw they were broken, and then slid them into the chest pocket of his olive green jacket. But then Pat turned toward the gunman, his jaw clenched. The gunman pulled the gun's hammer back with his thumb and returned the barrel to the co-pilot's neck. Pat slowly raised his hand, slid back the right side of his headphones, and yelled,

"And then what?"

The gunman grinned as he slowly released the hammer on the gun and handed Pat a third card.

COORDINATES ARE ON THE REVERSE SIDE.

4,000-FOOT PAVED RUNWAY.
LAND. TAXI TO WHITE VAN.

SPIN THE PLANE AROUND FOR TAKE-OFF.

SET BRAKES. THROTTLE TO IDLE.

EVACUATE THE PLANE.

**NOBODY WILL GET HURT
UNLESS YOU DEVIATE.**

**DO AS YOU ARE TOLD, AND
EVERYONE GOES HOME.**

**TELL PASSENGERS YOU ARE
LANDING IN FIVE MINUTES.**

**DO NOT CONTACT ANYONE.
DO NOT TRY ANYTHING.**

YOU WON'T BE THE FIRST PERSON I'VE SHOT.

Pat flipped the card over, read the coordinates, and handed the card to Charlie. The gunman studied both men, watching for them to disobey orders and try something, confident that the other gunmen aboard would follow orders and wreak havoc if needed. He watched as Pat shrugged his shoulders at Charlie and hit the switch to flash the auxiliary lights that ran the length of the plane's interior, a signal for passengers to return to their seats, buckle up, and plug in their headsets. He waited for a minute and then announced a change of plans.

"Well folks, this seems to be your lucky day," Pat began. "This happens now and then. There's absolutely nothing to worry about, but we need to put her down at a nice little runway near here to check the oil pressure in one of our engines." Pat looked across the cockpit at Charlie, who shrugged his shoulders and nodded his approval.

"How's that make you lucky? Well, instead of one take-off and landing, you'll get two today for the price of one. Once we land, we'll turn her around for take-off, and after we come to a full stop, we'll ask you to hang your headsets, unbuckle, and head to the rear of the plane, where your fine co-pilot Charlie Taylor will reset the ladder, and help you off the plane. The engines will remain at idle, and the props will be turning, so I need you to put your phones and cameras away; you will need to pay attention. Keep both hands free for the ladder, walk directly around the horizontal stabilizer, the plane's tail, and head to a white service van where we'll ask you to sit tight until we know we're ready for the next leg of this adventure."

Having retaken his seat just past the waist gunner position on the plane's starboard, Benny Armstrong shook his head at his son John as they listened to the captain's message. John raised his hands in the air as Benny first looked at the concerned faces of the young couple across from them and leaned in toward John.

"Something's not right," Benny yelled. "That guy who ran past us must have found something wrong with the plane. I've never heard of this happening before." John shook his head in disagreement and yelled his response.

"That's part of the surprise, Pop; I paid extra for this." Benny studied his son's face. He'd known his son's expressions since he was a baby and knew he was joking away the tension, or at least trying to. John shrugged his shoulders and forced a smile.

"It's not like we can do anything about it. These guys are pros. They'll get us on the ground, and we'll figure it out there." John unbuckled, moved to the waist gunner window, and studied the two starboard engines. Then he stepped across to the port side and did the same. He gave the couple a thumbs-up and sat down beside his father.

"I don't see any smoke or anything leaking," John called out. Benny shook his head and put on the face that he had shown his son for years, the expression that said, *It'll be okay*. Benny turned and looked across at the young couple holding hands. He saw the concern in their eyes, smiled, and then shouted at them.

"This happens all the time—nothing to worry about. Go back to taking pictures and enjoying this. It's a once-in-a-lifetime adventure, so enjoy every minute of it." The couple returned his smile but still seemed on edge. But then Benny noticed something. He waved to the couple and shouted as they lifted their headsets. Benny pointed to the empty belly gun turret.

"It's a shame to miss out on that view; you should climb in." Christa laughed and shook her head. "No way!" She smiled at Benny as Walt nudged her with his elbow.

"It's weird," he shouted. "I've been trying to Facetime some of this, but there's no signal." Like Benny, Christa shrugged her shoulders and surveyed the plane's interior.

He studied the .50 caliber on his side of the plane and thought of how scared the young men must have been who stood in these spots all those years ago, so far from home. So vulnerable. So scared. So courageous. He focused on his son, who stared blankly at the belly turret. *Maybe they need to stop flying some of these rare birds,* Benny thought. *Just stepping into one of these, into this hallowed space, should be enough.*

Suddenly, the captain's voice caught Benny's and the other passengers' attention.

"Okay, folks. I hope everyone's got their cameras and phones ready. We'll be touching down in one minute. Remember, once we come to a complete stop, the co-pilot will walk through the plane. Put your cameras and phones in your pockets or backpacks. Follow him to the exit, keep close to the tail, and walk straight to the white van."

∽

Pat and Charlie did as they were directed in the cockpit at gunpoint. They brought the warbird down gently onto the tarmac runway and taxied toward the white Ford passenger van parked just as the gunman's note had said. With no tower, hangars, or support vehicles in sight, Pat wondered who would put a runway in the middle of nowhere. But that didn't matter now. What would happen next was the big question. He had done as the bastard holding the gun had directed, running every possible scenario through his head of how this might end. He knew how it should; if only the pistol he kept in the glovebox of his car was with him now instead of in a parking lot back at the Palm Springs airport.

∽

The gunman held the gun in his right hand, tapped Charlie on the arm with the barrel, and motioned for him to follow. He backed across the catwalk, slid the gun inside his jacket, and stopped at the radioman's station. As far as he could tell, the two seniors remained seated throughout the flight. He smiled and gestured for them to walk to the plane's rear. As they did, their legs initially moved slowly but quickened within a few steps. He kept an eye on the flight crew and watched as Charlie stepped down onto the catwalk. He withdrew the gun, stepped back against the radioman's desk, yelled for Charlie to get moving, and shoved the co-pilot past him when he grew close.

"Get everyone the hell off this plane. Now!" Then the gunman spun and returned focus and his aim toward the pilot.

"Let's go!" the gunman yelled and then watched as Pat stepped down from the cockpit. "Get moving," the gunman yelled as he gestured with the gun, but the pilot didn't move.

"What about the two in the nose? We need to evacuate them, too," Pat shouted. The gunman shook his head.

"They're with me."

✧

Minutes later, as the passengers and crew emerged one by one from the B17's starboard hatch, the older men who had quietly occupied the radioman's station struggled to find their footing as Charlie guided them down the aluminum ladder. They acknowledged Charlie's hand gestures, kept hold of their hats, and walked close to the plane's tail and toward the white van. Pat and then the gunman were the last to exit the plane, walking directly behind the pilot, using the man's body to obscure the view of his gun. As they approached the van, suddenly, the rear door opened, and a short, stocky figure dressed in black fatigues and wearing sunglasses and a black cap stepped out and onto the ground carrying a long, black case. He set it on the ground, returned to the back of the van, removed a large black gear bag, and placed it alongside the case.

"Must be a mechanic," Walt said as he regarded the man and continued walking.

In the bright sunlight, while nothing else could seem out of the ordinary at this point to most, only those with keen eyes noticed what would soon concern them all. The figure wore a holstered weapon on his left hip and had a small black assault weapon on a sling across his chest. The figure began to walk toward them, waving for them to head toward the front of the van. As the six paying customers began to slow, they quickly became aware of what was happening. Some stopped but were soon pushed from behind them as the lead gunman shouted.

"Move!"

Walking alongside his father, John Armstrong slid his phone from his pocket and attempted to make a phone call. Without warning, the gunman at the van fired a short burst over the group's heads, a shower of brass clinking on the tarmac. Some froze, others dropped to the ground.

"No phones!" the man yelled, lowering the barrel toward the Armstrongs.

Pat cringed as the weapon fired but kept walking, turning every few feet to look back at the B-17 he'd been forced to abandon. The anger boiling inside was matched by the guilt and helplessness crushing him.

CHAPTER TWO

As THE SIX passengers and two pilots huddled near the front of the van, the gunman from the plane nodded to his accomplice, who then disappeared behind the van, returning with a drone and a black canvas gear bag.

"Phones, smart watches, wallets, IDs, cameras, all go in the bag," the man shouted, but nobody moved. Instead, the passengers looked at each other and to their flight crew for something, guidance, an explanation, or perhaps a rescue of some sort. Another burst from the assault weapon made everyone jump, and within seconds, the gear bag was full of phones and would soon be attached to the drone. The plane's gunman stepped close to the man from the van. They fist-bumped and then waved at the plane. Everyone followed their gaze and stared back at the B-17 until moments later, a third man, dressed like the others, exited the plane and ran toward them carrying something other than a gun.

"Is that what I think it is?" Charlie asked Pat as the man approached the drone.

"Damn it, they removed the transponder."

The group stood helplessly and watched as the third man placed the object into the gear bag and ran back to the plane.

"Okay, everybody, get inside the van. There's a cooler in the back with water and a map on the dash on how to get back to Palm Springs. There's also a tracker and microphones inside. If you stop anywhere, we will know it and respond. If you attempt to flag down or contact law enforcement or anyone else, we will know it, and if you do, someone you care about will bleed. The rest of my team are watching Mrs. Armstrong, Mrs. Taylor, some poodle named Precious, and all the rest," the gunman stated. Suddenly, John Armstrong stepped forward. He glared at the pilot and co-pilot and then returned focus to the lead gunman.

"This is bullshit. You're bluffing."

The gunman from the van raised his assault weapon and pointed it not at John but at Benny instead.

"When you purchased your rides and filled out those wavers online, we found out where you lived and what matters to you. Still living with your parents at your age, Johnny boy. Really? Nobody needs to get hurt, especially me and my team, so get in the van and drive back to Palm Springs." He pointed at the drone.

"That is going to fly there, making it look like the plane may have lost its radio but is still headed home with your phones showing your loved ones you're headed that way too if they're tracking you, and you can retrieve your stuff when you get back. Now, unless someone wants to be a hero, get moving." Pat stepped away from the group as he fought back his rage and waved for everyone to get into the van.

"What if we need to use the bathroom," Walt called out. Some of these passengers are older, and she can't pee into a plastic bottle." Christa elbowed him. "Shut up." The lead gunman laughed. Suddenly, the man with the Phillies hat spit tobacco chew on the ground.

"Hell, boy, this wouldn't be the first time I pissed out the window of a moving vehicle."

"There's an orange utility bucket with a lid in the back," the second gunman told them. "That'll have to do."

"Come on, let's get going," Pat said, turning toward the ring leader. "I have no idea what this bastard has in mind, but he's letting us go, so let's do just that." Charlie was the first to climb in, taking the front passenger seat and slamming the door closed as the others boarded through the side doors. The gunman stepped toward Pat.

"You're a smart man." Pat just stared.

"And what now? What are you going to do with her?" Pat asked.

"She'll be in good hands. The two riding in the nose have flown these before, so don't worry. But say goodbye. You'll never see her again." The gunman stepped closer. "Now go." Pat paused as he took a long look at the warbird and felt like he was saying goodbye to an old friend he'd never see again. Then, prodded by the barrel of a gun, he climbed into the driver's seat, put the van in gear, and drove off. Inside, Charlie and the others turned in their seats and watched as the drone took off and the three men in black ran toward the B-17.

"You should turn around and run them the hell over," Charlie shouted, but Pat ignored him.

"Pat, we can't just let them take her!" he shouted in frustration.

"Picture Linda lying in your kitchen with her throat slit. Is that worth the risk?" Pat shouted as he looked in the rearview mirror and watched the B-17 gain speed as it raced down the runway. He slammed on the brakes and opened the door. He stood on the doorstep, watched her climb, and bank to the right. Suddenly, a voice sounded over the van's speakers.

"If you stop again, people will die. Last warning."

Pat sat down in his seat, put the van back in drive, and sped away.

❧

From inside the plane, the man from the van was now seated in the tail gunner's position and radioed the new pilot.

"The drone's on course, and so are they," he reported. "They'll be pissing into the empty water bottles, I'll bet. No way that guy's stopping until they get back to the airport."

From his position at the radioman's desk, the ringleader monitored the California State Patrol and Arizona Highway Patrol communication systems and any broadcasts from the Palm Springs airport.

"No mention of anything having to do with this bird," he radioed the two in the cockpit and his tail gunner. "You know the drill. Fly fast and low, and we'll swap her out for a big bag of money in about thirty minutes. Keep watching for small planes who might take an interest in us." He looked across the cabin at the open gear bag on the floor. The two assault rifles, extra magazines, and plate carriers – what civilians call bulletproof vests- were ready – just in case. His gaze then went to the long hard case and the long gun he'd brought aboard. He'd double-checked it just before wheels up, chambering a round in the high-caliber hunting rifle. If any pilots came within sight, they'd be the first plane ever shot out of the sky by an American warplane over the United States."

From the cockpit, Jay Wilkins and Lester Jones, two pilots who had flown cargo aircraft, most times with illegal cargo onboard, all across South America and the African continent, nodded as they listened to the ringleader's message.

"One thing, though," Wilkins said into his mic.

"What?" the ringleader responded.

"Witnesses. You left witnesses." At his radioman's seat, the ringleader smiled as he inspected the gun he'd used to take over the aircraft and then looked down at the bulge in his black jeans above the ankle.

"That was the deal. Nobody gets hurt unless it's necessary; it wasn't, and as I've told you before, I'm a man of my word." The ringleader smiled as he returned his gaze to his black jeans and uncrossed his legs.

On the ground, hikers in the Arizona desert were racing to the top of a hill. As the young woman reached the top, she raised her hand with pride and shouted she'd won, beating her two friends from work who had stumbled in the sandy soil. Then, in a flash, she screamed and dove to the ground as something green or perhaps olive, its massive engines roaring like lions, flew low and just over her. As she looked up and brushed the dirt from her face, the object disappeared from view as quickly as it had arrived.

The olive skin of the vintage warbird was a stark contrast to the desert landscape beneath them. As it landed and then taxied toward the large tan and brown Quonset hut-style hangar, it contrasted the modern, state-of-the-art pearl white Global 6500 jet with the black and gold stripe adjacent to it. Then, as Wilkins idled the warbird straight inside the building, a set of doors quickly closed, which forced those aboard to struggle momentarily as their eyes went from bright daylight to near darkness. Inside the warbird, the ringleader tensed.

"Now, if they keep their side of the bargain, everyone here gets to go home."

CHAPTER THREE

Squinting as he drove west into the blinding sun, Pat clenched the wheel and thought of his broken aviators lying back in the warbird he'd surrendered. He'd worn them for a million air miles, perhaps more, over the years.

"I'll tell you what, those bastards are smart," he said as he looked at Charlie.

"Charlie?" After a moment, the co-pilot, now riding shotgun in the van, shook his head.

"They killed the radio, so we couldn't find out what was happening."

"And the more I think of it, I'll bet they bought up the rest of the seats to limit the number of passengers they'd have to deal with." From the back, John agreed.

"So what do you think they'll do with her?" Pat looked at John in the rearview mirror and shook his head.

"God only knows. Maybe once we stop, we'll learn that whatever's going to happen already has."

"Damn it, we should have done something," Charlie said as he slammed the dashboard. "We're going to be laughingstocks. We handed over a B-17 without putting up a fight."

Pat stared at his friend in disbelief. *That's what you're worried about?*

"You realize we should have landed there a long time ago," Charlie said. "Even if that drone did what that bastard said it would, they'd have sent out choppers and planes by now looking for us. This place is going to be a damn circus when we arrive. Linda's probably been notified, and if she has, with her high blood pressure, I'll be shocked if she hasn't had a stroke."

In the second row, in the window seat on the driver's side, Benny had scribbled notes and passed them back and forth with the pilots up front. Some of his suggestions caused Pat to shake his head a few times, but one that read, *You did good back there, skipper,* caused Pat to give Benny a nod and a wink in the rearview mirror. To his surprise, nearly all the passengers slept for most of the ride until he woke them.

"Okay folks, the next exit, down Gene Autry Trail, and we're there," he called out.

As they approached the gates, Charlie had been right. There were crowds of people, news vans, fire & rescue equipment, jammed traffic, and more. Finally, Pat pulled onto the shoulder of the road, got out, and suggested the rest stay put until he could communicate with the proper authorities, who could then usher them into the facility and the relative safety of the air museum where everyone's day had started. East of there, the ringleader and his team stepped from the warbird they had been hired to acquire and walked toward a feeble man in a wheelchair, his nurse, and Diane Fleming, the stunningly beautiful middle-aged blonde with the German accent who had arranged it all.

"You did it," she gushed, congratulating the man and his team. In the near darkness, three of the four had remained behind and close to the short aluminum ladder near the plane's tail. Only the ringleader stepped forward into the light.

"Yes, as promised," he told her, then focused on the man in the chair. The man seemed confused, with tears in his eyes, and unable to speak.

"Now your grandfather will get his wish." The woman smiled and gestured for the nurse to wheel her charge back into the darkness while she concluded their business. She snapped her fingers, and out of the shadows behind her, a tall, fit man wearing a blue suit, white shirt, and blue tie approached and placed a small black canvas gear bag on the cement floor. As he stepped back into the darkness, the ringleader took a knee, unzipped the bag, studied the contents, and looked back at his team, smiling from ear to ear. Slowly, he looked at the woman, starting at her black designer heels, firm, tanned legs, athletic figure, and captivating eyes.

"Your vehicles and drivers are behind the building as arranged. So now, if you're eyes have enjoyed themselves enough, our business is concluded – for now." The ringleader stood up, lifted the bag, and extended his hand.

"Until we hear from you then," he said. She ignored his hand and then cocked her head.

"You didn't have any trace of an accent when we first met," Fleming said curiously. "Now, what is that I detect?" The ringleader cleared his throat and grinned.

"Things aren't always as they seem," he said, turned and motioned with his head for his team to follow him, and the four walked under the starboard side of the B-17, through an exit door, back into the blinding sunlight of the hot Arizona desert.

Fourteen hundred miles east of Palm Springs, a retired Marine, Chris Boone, pulled his old gray Toyota pickup off Interstate 10 and stopped in front of a convenience store needing a pit stop and some caffeine. He'd just flown to Houston from the Arabian Gulf, working three months on and one month off as a roughneck on offshore oil rigs. The eighteen hours in the air had worn him thin, but he needed to get home to San Antonio. His ailing father's health had continued its decline, and nothing was going to stop him from getting home to see him. As he stepped to the counter to pay for the large coffee, bag of Cheetos, and a milk chocolate Hershey bar, he was stunned at the Breaking News displayed on the TV behind the cashier.

B-17 WARBIRD STILL MISSING IN CALIFORNIA.

Chris shook his head in disbelief, paid for the goods, and then headed for his pickup, stopping to hold the door for an older man walking for the door slower than two teenagers whose jeans were half down their butts were willing to wait. As the two began to push past the senior citizen, Chris stuck out his foot and tripped the first one through the door.

"Dude, you okay? You must have tripped on your pants."

Shocked, the second teen started to yell at Chris, who calmly placed his goods on top of the counter, cracked his neck once and then again, and stared at the youth.

"You kiss your mom with that mouth?" Chris asked. The teen helped his friend up off the floor and responded. "Sure, right after I kissed yours."

"Really? She's dead, so that's pretty sick." The teens seemed stunned by the remark and stared at Chris, perhaps taking time to study the size and shape of the man refusing to give them way. Chris watched as the two seemed to consider their options.

"Walk away. I need to get on the road instead of screwing with you two." He watched their minds race and ended the incident as quickly as he'd started. He lurched at them and laughed as they both ran from the front of the store toward the McDonald's next door. He felt someone tug at his arm and tensed but relaxed when he saw the senior smiling.

"Thank you." Chris shook the man's hand, grabbed his purchases, and headed for his pickup. Once back on I-10, he dialed his SIRIUS radio to Fox News. Hearing a commercial playing, he tuned to CNN, hoping to hear more about the stolen warbird. With two hundred miles to go, he'd have plenty of time to catch up on all he'd missed back home. Nearly three hours after he chowed down on cheddar, chocolate, and caffeine, Chris texted Norma, his father's live-in nurse. When she'd responded, his father Leo was resting comfortably. Instead of heading straight home, Chris checked his watch and drove directly to the local roadside bar he'd first learned to do shots in before shipping off with the Marines twenty years ago. He stretched as he stood up from the driver's seat and cracked his aching back. He knew what would make that feel better, what would make everything feel better: cold beer and lots of it. Chris grabbed the first bar stool, dropped two twenties on the bar, and waved for service. Then, he noticed the TV behind the bar. The local eleven o'clock news led the broadcast, showing aerial stock footage of the missing B-17 and the headshots of the pilot and co-pilot, Pat Monahan and Charlie Taylor. News like this was big in a town like San Antonio, with more military bases than professional ball teams. Someone had stolen something special, something hallowed, and they needed to be dealt with hard and fast. Behind him, someone else was focused on the news in a corner booth.

Liz Tyler slid back into the booth, placed a beer in front of her lover, Mark Childress, and handed Will Boone a soft drink. She and Mark returned their focus to the news.

"Is it diet?" Will asked. Liz shook her head no.

"One of these days, I'll get it right." She watched as Will pushed the drink away and played a game on his phone.

"You'll never guess who just took a seat at the bar," she said. At first, to her surprise, Will ignored her remark but suddenly looked up.

"It better not be Kathy Cross. That girl's crazy." Liz shook her head no.

"See for yourself," she said, motioning with her head.

"Shit," Childress said as he recognized the new arrival. "It's your damn brother."

She watched her brother's face brighten as he spun around in his seat, suddenly jumping up and walking straight for the bar. She watched as Will grabbed an empty beer bottle from a table and snuck up behind Chris, slowly pressing the mouth of the bottle against his brother's back.

∽

Chris moved his focus from the TV once it switched from the B-17 to the local weather and surveyed the female patrons around the bar. Suddenly, he tensed as he felt an object press against his spine. He felt someone's breath against his neck as they uttered a command.

"Don't move!" Then, without blinking, Chris spun on his seat, knocked the bottle from the assailant's hand, spun the threat where he stood, and wrapped him in a stranglehold that caused the assailant to utter, "Uncle!" Chris loosened his grasp slightly and whispered in Will's ear.

"No, I'm your big brother." Chris released his grasp, spun Will back around, and wrapped his arms around him in a bear hug as he lifted him off the floor.

"One of these days, big brother, one of these days," Will managed to deliver as he gasped for air. Chris laughed as he released Will. There were ten years between them, and they'd often joked, as did their friends, that their mother must have received a special delivery from the mailman because the two couldn't have looked more different. Often admired for his charisma, Chris, at forty, had maintained the same fit physique he'd had playing quarterback in high school football. The 210 pounds of muscle still hung well on his six-two frame, and his piercing blue eyes had intrigued women and lasered fear into adversaries for years. At thirty, Will couldn't have been more different. At just under six foot and weighing a scant 140 pounds, his dark brown eyes and pale skin had left many to look at him as almost sickly, which made him feel awkward more often than not. Chris smiled at his brother as tears wet his eyes. He waved to the bartender.

"More beer for me and a Diet Coke for my bro!" Chris sat, and Will stood close, his arm on Chris' shoulder.

"When did you get back?"

"An hour ago, I guess. Home for a few weeks to see everyone and then off to Kuwait again." Chris and Will lift their drinks and clink glasses.

"How's Pop?" Chris asked and then watched as the enthusiasm in his brother's face melted away.

"You staying out of trouble like you promised?" Chris asked, hoping the change of topic might help, and it seemed to. He watched his brother perk up with excitement.

"Sure am. I'm doing a lot of side jobs. We even did a Make-A-Wish come true for an old veteran. It made me feel really good." Chris took a drink as he smiled with pride.

"Really? What did you do?" As Will was about to answer, Chris saw his expression change again. This time, fear filled him as Chris watched his eyes, knowing someone was approaching from behind him.

"Let me guess. I can smell it. A piece of shit just dropped in." Chris turned on his stool to see Mark Childress standing close.

"Yep. Well, there goes the neighborhood," he said with disgust. "It's Mr. Dishonorable Discharge himself." Childress gritted his teeth.

"Never going to let that one go, are you?" Childress said through a clenched jaw. Chris turned back to Will, a look of disappointment flooding his expression.

"You're not still hanging out with this asshole?" Will didn't answer, and that said it all.

"Damn it, Will!" Suddenly, Childress put his hand on Chris' shoulder, which was the worst thing he could have done to this tired and frustrated Marine. In the blink of an eye, Chris spun and rose from his seat, knocking the arm from his shoulder and dropping Childress to the grimy bar floor with a brutal forearm to the chest. Just as quickly as Will had jumped back, knocking his stool to the floor, Liz arrived and reached for Chris, who immediately grabbed her by the throat with his right hand and kept her at arm's length as he brought the brown hiking boot on his left foot down hard on Childress' throat.

"Either of you move, and I crush it," he declared. Liz reached for a beer bottle on the bar as Childress struggled. Chris tightened his grasp on her as he pressed harder on Childress and grinned as she placed both hands up in sur-render, and her lover on the floor also gave in. Neither of them moved, and then a familiar voice called out to Chris as patrons stepped away or headed for the exit.

"Hey Chris, when'd you get back," the voice said from behind him.

Chris turned and smiled with surprise at his Marine buddy turned San Antonio police detective Billy Brad-shaw. He kept his foot in place on Childress and tightened his grasp on Liz as she tried to free herself. Bradshaw came closer and stopped alongside Chris.

"Either of them have a weapon?" Bradshaw asked.

Chris shook his head no as he put more weight on Childress, who was struggling for breath.

"Either of them threaten you in any way?" Bradshaw asked as he surveyed the bar; the look he gave the regulars who had remained to watch the show must have achieved its goal as each of them quickly turned their focus elsewhere. Finally, Chris took a deep breath and answered.

"Well, the stench from the shit on the floor is pretty offensive, and if you were to check, I'm sure you'd find a knife or maybe some drugs on at least one of them." Bradshaw placed his right hand on Chris' shoulder, which had resulted in violence moments before, but not now.

"Come on, Chris, turn them loose before someone puts us on the internet." Chris laughed.

"That'll never happen, not in this bar." Bradshaw shook Chris' shoulder and stepped closer.

"Come on, bud, save me some paperwork and you a night in jail. Turn them loose and then shake the shit off your boot." Chris let out a breath and then stepped back, freeing Childress and Liz from his hold. He turned to find Will standing a few feet away and watched him retake his seat, turning his back to all of them. He heard Childress and Liz coughing and clearing their throats and took a defensive stance just in case the two were interested in another dance. Bradshaw stepped between them.

"Either of you have an open tab?' he asked. Liz shook her head no as Childress spit on the floor close to the detective's feet. Bradshaw placed his hands together, interlocked his fingers, and cracked his knuckles.

"Really? Now you two need to head home, wherever the hell that is, and don't let me find you sitting in the

parking lot. A lot of bad stuff can go down in the dark."
Chris watched as his friend stepped on the spit and came
nose to nose with Childress.

"You feel me?" Childress seemed ready for a fight, but
Liz took his arm.

"Come on, we can do this some other time." Childress
shook off her arm and stormed for the door. As he passed
Will, he called out.

"You coming?" Chris spun and glared at Will. It
only took a second for his brother to muster an awkward
response as he fidgeted while rubbing his neck. "No, I'll
stay. I haven't seen him in a long time." Chris and Bradshaw watched as Childress stormed from the place with
Liz in hot pursuit. They stood there quietly, watching the
door for a minute in case anyone had second thoughts.
Then, they heard a car's tires screaming from the parking lot onto the access road out front and speeding away.
Chris gave Bradshaw a friendly push.

"I had that," he told the detective. Bradshaw turned
and shook his head.

"Still as much of a hothead badass as the day you
retired from the Corps." Chris shook his head no. "You
mean the day *we* retired. Now sit down and let me buy
you a drink." Bradshaw frowned.

"Hell no, I'm still working," Bradshaw said as he
waved to the bartender.

"So what are you doing in here then?"

"I saw your truck outside." The bartender took Bradshaw's order, two Diet Cokes and another beer for Chris.

"How's your dad doing?" Bradshaw asked. Chris
shrugged his shoulders, turned to face Will, and raised

his brow for an answer. Will shook his head and then turned away.

Down the road, Childress slid his black late model BMW sedan to a stop in the empty parking lot of an abandoned car dealership. Then, he got out of the car and opened the trunk. Liz got out quickly and met him there.

"What are you doing?" Liz shouted as Childress pulled two pistols from a gear bag and held them up, one in each hand.

"Are you crazy," she shouted. "You can't go back in there, and you can't follow him home. Put those away and get back in the car." Childress glared at her, shouted something unintelligible, and then did as he was told.

"That's the last time that prick puts his hands on me. One of these days, I'm going to kill that son of a bitch." Childress watched as Liz shook her head, pulled a joint from her black leather vest pocket, and lit it. As Liz watched, he checked his hair in the mirror and slammed the steering wheel with his hands. She took a hit and passed it to Childress, who initially waved it off.

"Come on, you need to chill, but you also need to use your head." He stared at her and then the smoking joint, taking it from her and taking two long hits before handing it back. As he exhaled, he asked, "Okay, so what does that mean?" Liz took another hit and then threw it out the window.

"All those jobs we get off the dark web. There are plenty of killers on there. From dipshits needing to make a fast buck to former special ops guys using what the military taught them. You should see what some of them charge. We need to use one of them to take out that bastard and the cop, too, if necessary." Childress stared at her; he'd begun to feel the effect of whatever they'd just smoked and wanted more. She shook her head no.

"You need to steer clear of them. Hell, you made thirty grand this week in cash. Let me find someone to get Chris off your back forever." Childress stared at Liz as if suddenly remembering how smart and hot she was. He leaned across the console and took her by her long black hair. She placed her hand on his lips.

"And with Chris gone and their pop on his way out, that gullible little autistic's going to need us even more."

"What about their sister?"

"One thing at a time."

Childress moves her hand from his mouth and leans closer, but she pulls away.

"Okay, go ahead. Make it happen," he says. She smiles and then climbs over the console as he reclines his seat.

CHAPTER FOUR

STANDING OVER THE sink in the modest kitchen where he was raised, Chris covers his eyes as the morning sun sends lightning bolts to the crushing hangover he woke up with. He turns his back to the light and stares at the old Mr. Coffee maker, begging it to brew faster. Suddenly, Norma, the young, attractive, hospice caregiver who has looked after the declining Leo Boone for much longer than anyone had expected, looked after him for nearly a year, enters and greets him with a big hello. He watched as she covered her mouth and laughed as she realized she'd come upon a wounded animal – him.

"How is he this morning?" he asks in a near whisper. She looks at the coffee pot, removes two mugs from the overhead cabinet, fills them both, and hands one to Chris.

"He has the constitution of a bull elephant, but I think he is nearing the end." Chris smiled at the comment, thanked her for the coffee, and then went to spend time with his dad.

At first, he just stood in the doorway and stared at what was left of the indestructible hero who had raised him, the man who had taught him to be strong, protect the innocent, be a man of your word, and never – ever hurt a woman. His hero, now unconscious and frail in the hospital bed that had displaced the queen his parents shared for years. As Chris entered the room, he pulled a chair close to his father's bedside, placed his hand on his dad's, and said softly, "Hey Pop. I'm home." Hoping for a response of some sort, anything, a change in his breathing, a flicker, anything, but none came. He grasped his dad's hand and held it tight. After a few minutes, still holding his hand, Chris surveyed the room he and his brother Will had run into so many times growing up; Chris, mostly to let Mom know his team had won another game, and Will, much less enthusiastically, living with the challenges he was born with. Chris smiled as he studied every item on his late mother's bureau, every plaque or trophy he'd brought home from playing ball, his sister Susan's awards from running high school track, and Will's ribbons from his tenacity and success running cross country. He paused, squeezed his father's hand, and then looked at his dad's pale green matching armoire. High atop it, there were only two items. An 8x10-inch framed color photo of Lilly Boone, his mom, and beside it, a plastic scale model of a B-17 Flying Fortress Leo and Chris had built together so many years ago after dinner at the dining room table. The model of what Chris' brave, young grandfather had flown in over Europe during World War II.

He could still smell the model glue and hear his mother, Lilly's warnings to protect her precious tabletop. Chris fought back tears as he turned his attention back to the man he adored, lying there before him. He leaned in.

"Pop. I'm here. It's okay. You don't have to keep fighting. You can let go now and be with Mom. It's okay. Susan and Will are fine, and we will always look out for him, no matter what." Chris squeezed his father's hand once more.

"It's okay, Pop. Just know that we all love you." Then, as he choked back his tears, Chris saw one form in his father's left eye. He squeezed his hand again and didn't let go. Then, hearing someone at the doorway, Chris wiped his face on his black t-shirt sleeve and turned toward it. There, Will stood, tears streaming down both cheeks.

"Hey, come on over. Pull up a chair and hold his other hand. He knows we're here." Will took one step in, then another, but suddenly, he turned and ran from the room, almost knocking Norma over as she arrived with fresh linen for their father's bed.

"It's time for me to bathe him and change his clothes and sheets," she said softly. Chris squeezed his father's hand and then let go.

"I'll be right back, Pop. Don't go anywhere," he said and then caught himself, help laughing. "Not till I come back."

Outside, he found Will staring into space, seated in one of three old rocking chairs that had decorated the porch for as long as he could remember. Chris approached him and placed his right hand on Will's left shoulder.

"You okay?"

"What do you think?" Will responded.

"Probably not. Your damn face is all wet." Will stepped away, laughing, wiping his tears, and then turned to his big brother.

"What am I going to do if he dies?" Chris took a step toward Will but saw him tense, instead taking a seat in the first rocker.

"He is going to die, Will. It's not if, but when. We've talked about this a lot. Susan has talked about it with you, too. We've talked about you being prepared for it."

"But where am I going to live?" Chris shook his head, unsure if he wanted to yell or laugh.

"Right the hell here, for as long as you want. The house is paid off, and Susan and I will always make sure the bills are paid and that you are safe and as happy as we can make your life."

Then, the sound of a vehicle coming up the drive made them both turn. It was their sister, Susan. She brought her white Ford pickup truck to a stop behind Chris' Toyota and approached the front steps.

"Well, speak of the devil," Chris shouted and stood up to greet her.

"I thought you were keeping an eye on him," Chris said as she reached the top step.

"Who, Dad? Norma's here twenty-four-seven." Chris shook his head no and turned toward Will.

"No, him – our baby brother."

"Well, hell, Chris, it's great to see you too. Welcome home, and when are you leaving?"

Chris reached down and wrapped his arms around her. At first, she tenses but drops her bag to the deck and hugs him back. After a moment, he steps away, holding her hands, and looks at her from shoes to hair.

"You look like a real professional." Susan frees her right hand and pokes him hard in the chest.

"I am a professional. I'm a Federal Prosecutor for the Western District of Texas, remember?" Chris acted confused.

"Oh yeah, I remember reading something about that."

"Very funny, you big dipshit," she said, reaching up and messing with his hair.

"You need a haircut, Marine." Chris stepped back and ran his fingers through his hair but turned serious when he read her expression.

"Norma called and said I should stop by. How is he?"

"You know the old man. He could live another ten years or be dead in there right now." Will kicks at one of the rockers.

"Don't say that!" Chris and Susan look at Will and shake their heads.

"Like I said, I thought you were keeping an eye on this guy." Susan took a step back and stared at him.

"As best I can. I have a huge caseload, and Norma lets me know if there's anything funny going on with him. Why?" Chris took a step toward Will, again shaking his head.

"Because he was sitting in a booth with Childress and his girlfriend last night at the bar." Chris turned, wanting to watch her reaction.

"What did I tell you about those two?" She shouted. Will shrugged and plopped down in the far rocker, away from them. Chris heard a growling noise from his sister, one he'd never heard before, and then watched as she picked up her bag and stormed into the house. Chris sat in the middle chair and rocked quietly, letting the chirping birds and the warm breeze calm him. Then, he turned to Will.

"Well?" Will rocked in his chair and began offering his defense.

"Liz finds jobs for me on the internet. Simple stuff. Helping people. I like doing that, especially if they're veterans like you, Pop, and Granddad." Chris studied his brother, trying to maintain his composure and hoping his vulnerable, often gullible brother was telling the truth.

"What kind of jobs/ Are you sure they're legal?" Chris watched as what looked like a sense of pride dressed Will's face.

"We just did one where we did a Make-A-Wish for a dying vet. He looked ancient. The guy was so happy he was crying the whole time. It was pretty cool." Will paused and appeared to calm. "It made me feel like I was doing something worthwhile." Chris smiled at Will.

"That's pretty cool. And where does Mark fit into all of this?"

"Sometimes, if Liz is busy, Mark drives." Chris struggled to keep the smile going.

"Okay, and where did this Make-A-Wish take place?" Then, just as Will was going to answer, Susan called out from inside the house.

CHAPTER FIVE

AT THE PALM Springs Police Department headquarters, Pat Monaghan sat impatiently on a metal chair at a cold metal table in a windowless interview room. He swirled what remained of his coffee in the paper cup as he stared at the mirror on the wall, wondering if it was one like he'd seen in the movies, with onlookers studying him. Then, seated across from him, a balding veteran detective, Jack Jones, loosened his Kelly green tie while his younger partner, Detective Molly Simms, played with her smartwatch.

"Okay, let's start over from the beginning," Jones suggested, but Pat wasn't having it. He tossed his now empty cup into the corner trash can and sat forward in his chair.

"Einstein had a definition for this," Pat stated with frustration. "It had something to do with insanity." Simms kept focus on her watch but spoke up.

"You know the drill. This smells, so we'll keep on you until you tell us the real story." Pat sat back in his chair and gave the mirror a passing glance.

"Already have. Ten times now. Some guy shoved a gun at us and directed us to land. He knew our names and where we lived. He knew Linda's name and the names of the passengers and their next of kin. My primary concern was for the safety of the passengers and our families."

"And you just landed where they told you to and got off. Nobody resisted?" Simms read from her notes. "And then you drove back to the airport without stopping anywhere to call for help." Pat cleared his throat.

"Read your notes. You seem to be pretty good at that."

Jones pushed back in his chair, the legs screeching on the tile floor.

"Those old warbirds are worth a fortune, aren't they skipper?" he asked. "Some might say since there's only a few left flying, B-17s that is, that they could be regarded as priceless."

"Hey, Simms, hand him your notes. We said that two hours ago." A loud knock suddenly interrupted them, and the door flew open. The detectives stared at the intruder while Pat turned and smiled.

"Hey, sis."

Pat's sister, younger by ten years, removed a worn, brown leather badge wallet from her suit coat and displayed it for the detectives. Simms stood up and leaned across the table to read it.

"Special Agent Linda Monaghan, Federal Bureau of Investigation. Phoenix, Arizona Field Office." Linda flipped the wallet closed and put it back in its place.

"Are you charging my brother with a crime?" Jones got up and extended his hand. Pat laughed to himself as he did.

"Don't make me tell you where to stick that detective; answer the question."

Jones forced a smile and then retook his seat.

"We're just making sure we understand exactly what happened out there. The pilot didn't rock the plane to disrupt the gunman. He's ex-military but didn't take any action or aggressive maneuvers to stop the incident and save the plane."

Linda looked down at Pat.

"Get up." Pat obliged her and stretched as his sister continued.

"Have you ever had a forty-five shoved into your neck or face?"

Simms looked at Jones. They both shook their heads no.

"Ever had the lives of a dozen people in your hands?" Jones stood up to protest.

"Now look, one has nothing to do with the other," he said defiantly.

Simms cleared her throat.

"Hey Pat," she began and waited for his attention. "Your co-pilot thinks you could have done more to save the plane." Pat was stunned by those words but refused to let it show.

"Did he?"

Linda shook her head, turned, and reopened the door.

"You coming? I'm hungry, and you're buying." Pat glanced one last time at the mirror and then smiled at the two detectives.

"Isn't she great?" he said, following Linda from the room.

❧

In the interview room, Simms and Jones sat quietly for a time.

"Now what?" Simms asked the senior detective, who shook his head as if he'd gotten water stuck in his ear. Simms laughed.

"You okay?" Jones ignored her question.

"We look for a grain of sand in a damn desert but head over to Parker first. They've found three bodies shot up and left in the desert."

"Related to this case?" Simms asked as she stood up.

"From what AHP reported, yes."

"But that's Arizona," Simms protested.

"Call it professional courtesy. Everybody wants that plane found. The sooner it's solved, the sooner all the resources can get back to things like drug smugglers, border control, and the really important stuff." Jones heads for the door and leaves without holding the door for her.

"What an asshole. Even I know how important that plane is."

CHAPTER SIX

Seated in a booth in their favorite Mexican restaurant in San Antonio, Chris sat across from Will and tore into his plate of food. The attractive waitress with flowing black hair and stunning brown eyes lingered, watching him feast, until a patron called for more sweet tea.

"You can't find anything like this in the Gulf," Chris said as he and Will fought over the last warm tortilla. Disappointed Will had given in so quickly, Chris just shook his head. They'd fought over tortillas there for years and hoped taking him would give them a chance to reconnect, but his brother seemed lost.

"How's your tacos?" he asked and shook his head in frustration when all he got in response was, "They're okay." Chris reached across to steal a taco and laughed as Will grabbed it.

"Hey, Pop's a tough son of a bitch. You never know; he might outlive us both." Will took a few bites of his food and washed it down with a diet soda."

"I doubt that. You're just trying to make me feel better.

You're never here, and warden Susan scared the crap out of me this morning." Chris shook his head in agreement.

"She got me too. I thought he was gone," Chris said as he fought back his emotion.

"And that's happened before. Susan thinks he stops breathing, so she screams and starts CPR, which makes things worse for Pop and scares the shit out of me." Chris sat back in the booth, surveyed the restaurant, and then waved at the server for another round of drinks.

"Wait, did you just call her warden?" Will nodded as he emptied his drink through a straw.

"Yeah, I did, and like I said, you're never around." Chris' mood changed. He knew Will was right but also knew he couldn't stand to be there for too long. It made him remember his wife, and that made him drink. He slammed his fork down on the table, glaring at his brother. He wasn't mad at him, though; he was angry at himself. A few male patrons seated nearby looked at Chris, who returned their look; the anger in his eyes forced them to turn away.

"Look, this is what I do. Susan's doing her thing, Norma's looking after Pop, and you're doing your thing. I just wish it wasn't with Childress and whoever he's with." Will smiled at the server as she delivered their drinks and removed the empties.

"Mark and I have been friends since high school. You know that. He always looked after me when someone picked on me, and I see him a hundred times more than I see you." Chris tossed his napkin on the table and got up.

"And that's what worries me."

Chris walked to the bathroom, chatting briefly with

the server as she cleared another table and entered the rest-
room. Once the coast was clear, Will pulled out his phone.

᷽

He sees a text from Childress. It reads:

> *We've got a job in Austin. Tonight.*

Will responds.

> *Chris is pissed.*

He looks up to ensure Chris isn't on his way and
watches as the text bubbles show that more is coming.

> *Screw him. I'm more of a big brother than
> he is. He's never here. Never been here for
> you like Liz and I have. Meet us at six.*

Will looks for Chris again and panics as he sees his
brother walking toward their table. Luckily, the server
steps in front of him and hands him a note, which gives
Will a second to send one last text and hide the phone.

> *Okay. See you at six.*

Then Will feels his brother's presence standing over
him. He looks up to see Chris, wearing a look of disappointment. Busted.

᷽

In Palm Springs, Linda Monaghan retracts the top on her
rented Ford Mustang convertible and drives out of the

police department parking lot as her brother Pat quickly fastens his seat belt and surveys the dashboard.

"Thanks for coming, but how did you know I was there?"

"It pays to have friends in law enforcement just about everywhere," she said as she accelerated through a yellow light.

"This thing's got some power." Pat sat quietly for a moment and watched in his sideview mirror for the lights of a police car that never came.

"So are you here on a case or?" Linda pulled into the parking lot of the Hilton hotel, stopped abruptly at the valet station, and tossed the keys to the attendant as she walked for the entrance. When she realized Pat hadn't followed, she turned to him.

"Hungry?"

Shortly after that, they were seated under an umbrella on the restaurant patio. After they ordered, she picked up where they'd left off.

"Once I saw you on the news, I put in for a week off and got on a plane. Thanks so much for not answering your phone for the last twelve hours." Pat laughed as he placed his phone on the table.

"It's still off. Once the reporters got my number, that thing exploded with texts, calls, and voicemails." Pat thanked a server as their coffees were delivered and then continued.

"You'll do almost anything to get me to visit, but this? This is over the top." Pat laughed.

"I'd say."

Linda studied her brother's face. She saw the mess the

incident had made of his emotions. She read anger, frustration, denial, embarrassment, and concern and shared that with him.

"I'd say."

"So where do you think they took her, and why?"

"Not sure. It could be a super-rich collector who has to have one. On the other hand, maybe someone who's had a run-in with someone at the museum, and this is payback. The bastards who took her treated her with care, though, so I don't think she's at risk as long as the pilots know what they're doing."

"So where could they have taken her?" she asked.

"Anywhere at this point, but they'd have to move her at night. They could jump from spot to spot and hope nobody sees them. With the right team and working fast, they could disassemble her and have her in a cargo plane or on a ship headed anywhere."

Linda had been with the agency for decades, first at the field office in Boston, then Charleston, Miami, and then Seattle before receiving her dream desk in Phoenix. She loved the desert, golf, the heat, and being closer geographically to her brother than ever before. She'd asked him to meet her halfway, maybe settle down in Scottsdale, but he'd told her more than once that he'd found a home in Southern California flying warbirds and teaching others how to fly and intended to stay put. Seeing the world with the United States Air Force and then with American Airlines, his version of retirement was to continue to fly but the planes that made him feel connected to their father, the warbirds he had flown during World War II.

"It was a ballsy move; I'll give them that," she remarked

as the server delivered their lunch. Suddenly, a man with a bald head and a beer belly dressed in a light blue golf shirt and tan khakis approached the table.

"You're that guy who lost the B-17," the man declared. Pat shook his head in disbelief as Linda pushed her chair back.

"Go away," she said sternly, but the man kept it up.

"Let me guess, you sold it, didn't you?" Linda slid her tan suitcoat back and tapped at the holstered black pistol on her hip. The intruder took a step back.

"Yeah, you're gonna need a bodyguard, you bastard," the man said, storming off.

Linda slid her chair back in close and watched Pat's face grow cold.

"That'll be the rest of my life if *I* don't get her back." Linda shook her head and reached across the table, placing her hand on his.

"You need to leave that to us, Pat. She's a national treasure. There will be a lot of law enforcement on the ground and in the air looking for her; at least, there should be. I've already heard some whining about budgets. But there will also be assholes like that one, ones carrying guns, who think it's their duty to find her too. You come across the wrong ones in the desert, and who knows what'll happen."

She watched as Pat cleared his throat, picked at his food, and smiled as she looked at her big brother with admiration.

"So, what time are you heading out?"

CHAPTER SEVEN

In San Antonio, Chris Boone sat quietly on the same barstool he'd warmed the night before, but it was much later, and the place was nearly empty. After he'd spent the afternoon at Leo's bedside, he did as he had so many times before; he drove to visit his wife, stopping to spend time at her grave as the sun touched the horizon. Then, sticking to his tradition, he needed a drink. Whenever he'd visited Cindy, the vibrant ER nurse killed by a drunk driver a year after Pat had retired from the Corps, he'd drink. Tonight, though, was different. Rather than pounding shots and beer, he nursed one and then another. Visiting his mother's grave had always been tough, but with Cindy now lying beside her, it tore at his heart and mind.

He sat there, politely ignoring the perky, blonde bartender's attempt at getting him to notice her, and thought of his wife, his sister, his brother, and then Leo, in that order. He thought of what life should have been like after retirement. Instead, he chose the life of a roughneck on oil rigs. "Won't fall in love on one of those," he'd tell his family and friends who questioned his choice. He knew another funeral was coming and wondered when it would come. Then, he waved to the blonde.

"Another beer," she asked. "How about a shot? On me, and I'll do one with you."

Pat smiled as he studied her angelic face and let his eyes move past her neck. He cleared his throat and shook his head.

"No thanks. Not tonight. I'll take a Red Bull instead." He didn't know it then, but that move might have saved his life.

For the first time, perhaps ever, Chris closed the place. He stood watch outside as the bartender and a server deadbolted the door and looked up at the blanket of stars as he waited for the two women to get to their cars and drive away safely. Then he heard a growl and realized he was hungry. He checked his watch as he walked toward his pickup and smiled when he realized the local Krispy Kreme would be open just long enough to grab a hot coffee and a box of warm glazed donuts and head home. Maybe he'd find Will still awake and up for a movie. Maybe Norma would join in. Perhaps he could place the open box near Leo and encourage him to smell the sweetness in the air. But then, without warning, something hard slammed across his upper back, and he fell face down onto the ground. Dazed for a moment, Chris felt someone jump onto his back. Then, they began smashing his head into the asphalt. It only took another second, but all his Marine training and his will to survive kicked in. He spun to his right, shifting the weight of his attacker from him, and then turned again, landing him on top. He pummeled the attacker's sides with hard elbow blows, right, left, and then right again. Then, as suddenly as the assault had begun, it was over. He stood up quickly, surveying the parking lot for additional threats, and looked down at the person who'd tried to kill him, lying there trying to catch his breath. He saw the piece of rusty angle iron the bastard had used on him and kicked it away. Chris was enraged and kicked the man hard in the side once and again, then took a knee and checked the person for weapons. To his surprise, the man swung at him from his spot on the ground, and Chris responded, knocking the man unconscious with a blow to the side of the head.

∽

The assailant regained consciousness but was dazed and even more confused. He couldn't move his arms or legs, but he smelled donuts. He tried to speak, but his mouth was taped shut. He tried to move his arms and legs, but they were restrained behind him with what felt like thin, plastic wire ties. He looked at his surroundings and finally realized he was tied up and lying in the back seat of a moving vehicle. Then, his captor, the man he had tried to kill, turned and smiled at him.

"Take it easy there, buddy boy. I'll have you home in no time."

The man shook his head again and felt for the wallet in his jeans pocket. It wasn't there.

∽

Finally, the ride south on Interstate 37 and then down State Road 181 was ending. Chris drove down a dirt road in Elmendorf toward a dark single-wide trailer, moving the truck to the left and right, allowing the headlights to scour the area. As he stopped and shut off the engine, he looked at the .45 caliber black Sig handgun in the console, closed the lid, and got out. He listened for a moment and enjoyed the quiet that calmed him. He looked up for the stars again but was disappointed to see clouds had their way across South Texas, ruining his view.

He opened the rear door.

"So I'll ask one more time. There's nobody else in there, right?" The man stared back at him, shaking his head no. Chris smiled, reached into the truck, and dragged the man out by his boots, letting gravity do the rest. The man cried out in pain through the tape.

"Hurts, doesn't it," Chris said as he studied the trailer and his surroundings again before pulling a large pocket knife and bending down to slice the ties on the man's ankles. He picked him up, shoved the man toward the front door, and stopped as they got close.

"Keys?" The man shook his head and tried to talk. Chris yanked the tape away.

"They're in my pocket, damn it." Without flinching, Chris kicked the door open and pushed the man inside. He flicked the light switch and groaned at the mess he'd just entered. There was a smell he couldn't recognize and was happy he couldn't: dirty cups and dishes in the sink, an overflowing trashcan full of beer cans, tequila bottles, and everyday trash. He spotted a lighter, needles, a tie-off band, and some drug residue on a table at the far end of the sofa. He grabbed the man by the arm.

"Where is it?" The man ignored his question, so Chris grabbed him by his long, greasy brown hair.

"Really? You want the rest of your teeth knocked out?" The man looked past Chris.

"On the kitchen table, under the towel." Chris smiled.

"You bathe? What a guy." Chris approached the table cautiously, removed the towel with two fingers, and tossed it on top of the dishes in the sink. There, as promised, sat an old dusty laptop. Chris tapped the mouse and grinned as the screen came alive.

"Password," he demanded. When he didn't hear a response, he turned and gave his host a threatening look.

"I'm a dead man, so go fuck yourself."

Chris responded with a laugh, pulling his knife from his jeans pocket again and stepped close.

"You're a drug addict, a shitty assassin, and a lousy housekeeper," Chris said as he brought the knife's blade to the man's ear. "I can get a tech to unlock this, so save me the time and save yourself more pain." The man shook his head, and then Chris grabbed the man by the hair, shoved him down on a worn sofa, shoved his knee into the man's chest, and placed the knife at the man's ear.

"Password," Chris demanded, hoping the man would relent. He'd done things like this and worse to terrorists back in Afghanistan and Iraq to secure intel, but he never liked it. It sickened him. He was all for delivering justice; he just didn't enjoy such methods. Chris looked around the room and saw a tequila bottle. He smiled.

"Give me the password, and I'll give you the tequila."

"Cowboys," the man whispered. "The password is Cowboys." Chris got up, cut the ties holding the man's hands, and gave him the bottle. He slid the knife back into his pocket and sat in front of the computer. As the man drank, Chris checked the history.

"A lot of Pornhub and what's this? You used Map-Quest to find the bar?"

"It's a big town."

Chris kept looking. Then he found it. "Makin' Money" was a site on the dark web where people found work, illegal work. He shook his head as he scrolled through the site. Beat up a cheating boyfriend. Steal something. Repo an engagement ring by any means. Hits like the one someone put out on Chris.

"Hell, that old airplane that got stolen out west. That was on there," the man said, the effect of a large amount of tequila in such a short time now slurring his speech.

"Show me. Show me who posted the hit on me," Chris said as he pulled the man up from the sofa and sat him down at the laptop. It didn't take long for the man to find the post. He clicked on it and sat back in the chair, pointing to the screen. Chris leaned in, repulsed by the man's breath.

"Almas Perdidas," Chris read, the screen name of the person who wanted him dead.

"What does it mean?" Chris asked.

"How the hell should," the man said abruptly until Chris cut him short with a hard tap to the head.

"Look it up!" The man typed away and then turned the laptop toward Chris.

"It means Lost Souls. They offered me a thousand dollars cash. Half up front, half when the job was done. They left it under a brick in front of your pickup truck at the bar. Chris stared at the screen and shook his head in disbelief.

"You've done this before?" At first, the man didn't answer but nodded as he took another drink.

"Well, they got what they paid for. That's what happens when you go cheap. Now, show me the airplane job – the one out west." The man just sat there; perhaps the reality of what was to come and a surge of alcohol was numbing his senses. Chris shook the guy.

"Show the airplane gig, and I'll leave." The man grumbled and moved the mouse until he found it.

"There it is, and now you can go, right?" the man said. Chris leaned in and was stunned by what he read.

"Almas Perdidas. The same people who put the hit out on me stole the plane." Chris sat back in his chair. He was confused, but the anger boiling up in him brought clarity.

"Where's the charger for the laptop?" The man looked around the room and pointed to the charger sticking out of a wall outlet.

"Get it," Chris demanded. As he did, Chris reached down and pulled a compact 9mm pistol from an ankle holster. In an instant, as the man tossed the charger on the table and sat down, Chris threw the towel over the hitman's head and shot him dead. Then, moving with precision, he holstered the gun, grabbed the charger, mouse, and laptop, and went outside to his truck. He returned to the trailer carrying a small metal gas can, quickly doused the kitchen with fuel, threw the open can down the hall into the bedroom, grabbed the lighter from the table, and stepped out. Without flinching, he flicked the lighter, tossed it inside, and returned to his pickup. He checked the wallet he'd thrown on the dash.

"Daniel Davis, Elmendorf, Texas," he said as he read the man's driver's license again and thought back to the bar parking lot. *How'd he get there? I didn't see any cars.* Chris removed the cash, counted out five crisp one-hundred dollar bills and a worn twenty, and slid the money into his back pocket. As the flames inside the trailer began to roar, he walked to the trailer door and tossed the wallet into the fire, followed by the ID. Once back in his truck, he drove off and watched in the mirror as the flames engulfed the trailer.

"Another lost soul who can't hurt anyone ever again."

On the ride home, he made peace with what he had just done. A killer was taken care of, and now Chris had something to work on. Something he could share with his cop friend Billy Bradshaw. Then, as he drove up the street toward his father's home, his heart began to race. The house lights were on, strange for this late at night.

CHAPTER EIGHT

As HE PULLED into the driveway, he knew. Susan's car was there at 4:30 a.m., which meant only one of two things. Will was in trouble again, or Pop had finally left them and gone to be with Mom. He shut off the truck and sat there, staring at the house. Tonight had been rough enough, and he didn't want the next chapter to begin. Not yet. After a few minutes, he took a deep breath and walked through the front door. In the hallway outside their father's door, Susan and Norma stood arm in arm. Susan slowly turned, her face red and her eyes swollen from tears.

"He's gone."

On the front porch, Chris and Susan sat quietly in the rockers while taking sips of coffee and relishing the sun's warmth as it rose higher and higher. They retold stories about their father and laughed until it hurt. Chris watched as Susan checked her phone.

"I can't believe he's not returning my messages," she said. "We had a deal. Keep the tracking on, and return my calls, no matter what." Chris nodded.

"Oh, and by the way, where were you last night? I left you messages, and your tracker was off, too. Did you two decide it was screw with Susan night or what?" Chris put his mug down on the deck and placed his hand on hers.

"No, I just had something to take care of." He squeezed her hand. "I'm sorry I didn't get here sooner." He looked at his sister and watched her expression morph from disappointed to concerned.

"By the way, you look like shit. Are you going to tell me what happened?"

"I got into something outside the bar last night. Some junkie jumped me, and."

The sound of a car racing down the street interrupted him, and they watched as a late-model black BMW sedan with tinted windows came to a fast stop at the edge of the property. The passenger side door slowly opened, and Will stepped out of the car. Chris zeroed in on his brother's expression. *He's busted, and he knows it.*

As quickly as the car had arrived, it pulled away, the tires screeching, and disappeared from Chris' view. Will stood in the street and finally began walking toward the house.

෨

As he got closer, he locked in on his sibling's faces. *Susan's been crying, and Chris looks like he's been fighting. Good, maybe the heat won't be on me for a change.* As he climbed the four front steps, he studied Chris' face.

"What's going on? You been in a fight?"

He watched as Chris squeezed Susan's hand, stood up, and approached him.

"Will, Pop finally lost his." The news hit Will like a truck. He knew the moment would come someday, just as it had with his mother, but he wasn't ready. He knew he never would be. He shouted "No" and ran into the house.

～

Susan got up from her chair and ran inside as Chris stood silently. He thought of his father and what they needed to do next. After that, he'd use that laptop in his truck to find out who wanted him dead and, with any luck, help find the missing B-17. He pulled his phone from his pocket, turned it on, and was on it with the funeral home minutes later.

Days later, in the quiet memorial park with rolling hills north of San Antonio, Chris stood alongside Susan and Will, reciting the Lord's Prayer with the forty or so mourners who joined them. In the distance, Chris saw the last two faces he wanted to see today – Childress and his Liz standing under a shade tree. He felt his jaw clench and then tighten even more. Luckily for them, the military honor guard began the ritual of folding the American flag that covered his father's oak wood casket. Chris watched as the flag was then handed to the U.S. Air Force Captain. As the man approached Susan, Chris studied the man's impeccable dress blue uniform, and silver buttons and thought of the much different one he had worn in the Marines. As the officer bent forward slightly and extended his hands holding the flag, he addressed her.

"On behalf of the President of the United States, the United States Air Force, and a grateful Nation, please accept this flag as a symbol of our appreciation for your father's honorable and faithful service." Then, as the captain turned and stepped away, a lone bugler played taps.

ॐ

Miles to the west of Texas, Pat Monaghan took the last sip of coffee from his thermos as he drove down one of what felt like a thousand state and county roads in desert Arizona. He checks the look of his new aviators in the mirror and shakes his head. *The other ones fit better.*

He pulled to the side of the road to recheck his Map-Quest and Garmin apps and was happy when he heard a familiar ringtone on his phone. His quest had taken him off of the media radar in Palm Springs, but the search had been hot and frustrating.

"He Sis. How's it going?"

"Striking out at every turn."

Pat put his white Jeep four-door in drive and got back on the road.

"Well, I'm not doing much better. I started with where we landed near Blythe, and I'm driving up and down every road out here just looking. I have a list of every known runway, and I've checked quite a few already, but no luck. Nada."

"Now listen to me. I'm serious. There's more out there in the desert than most people realize. Drug traffickers, people traffickers, bad guys who don't want to be found, and crazies with boundary issues. Drive onto the wrong property, and they'll shoot first and leave you for the birds." Pat smiled as he listened to his little sister. She might be with the FBI and be good with a gun, but she was still his little sister, no matter how much she proved otherwise.

"That's okay. I brought a few friends along, just in case."

"What? Who's with you? I thought just about everyone was treating you like a traitor."

Pat laughed despite the enormous pain he felt inside. He had been beating himself up with doubt and second-guessing for days and was surprised by how many friends had turned out to be the fair-weather kind.

"I've got Mr. Sig and Mr. Sauer with me, Linda," he said as he popped the center console and looked at the semi-automatic handgun and two boxes of ammunition he always kept handy, just in case." As he drove, he watched a red Peterbilt tractor-trailer coming from the opposite direction and felt the Jeep shake from the air the rig was pushing as it flew by.

"So, nothing on your end? No leads? Nobody saw or heard anything. It's kind of hard to miss a plane like that."

"Nope. Whoever did this was good, and despite everyone's efforts, we have nothing to go on. The police finally found the drone and the phones. The thieves rigged it and blew it up as it reached the golf course near the airport. The FBI lab has all that now, but they said, "Don't hold your breath."

∽

In Texas, Chris, Susan, Will, and Billy Bradshaw sat quietly in a large booth in the back of the same bar Chris frequented and had been assaulted outside of. They shared stories about Leo, their time in the Marines, Susan's track record for dating knuckleheads, and how proud their parents had been of Will's grades in school and his success running cross country. The blonde server, who usually tended bar, delivered another round of drinks, soda, and chicken wings and expressed her condolences a second time. Chris smiled and said thanks, but his attention was elsewhere. He was squinting to see the TV behind the bar. Susan turned to see what had caught his attention.

"Still no trace of her. No leads," she said as she read the scrolling news headlines. Bradshaw shook his head.

"Your granddaddy flew in one of them, didn't he?" Before Susan could answer, Will perked up with pride.

"He sure did. Was a tail gunner at only twenty years old."

Susan sipped her beer and said something that caught Chris by surprise.

"His sister's with the FBI."

"Who?"

"That B-17 pilot. I was just reading his bio on my phone."

Chris thought for a moment about what Susan had said, but then he saw Will's eyes grow, and he knew someone, more like something, was approaching their booth. Chris turned to see for himself just as Childress and Liz arrived. Chris began to get up, but Bradshaw was in the way and didn't budge.

"We know we're not welcome here, but I just wanted to say we're sorry about your father," Childress said, speaking directly to Will and then turned to Chris.

"Sorry about your father. You might remember I lost mine when I was a kid. You were lucky to have had

Leo as long as you did." Chris thought his jaw would explode as he exerted the pressure of a grizzly bear. He pushed at Bradshaw again and exhaled in frustration as his friend simply turned toward him and shook his head no. Then, Chris saw something. He stared at Childress and Liz's hands. They held them while they tried to talk with Will and didn't notice they were being studied. That was it! He could see ink on both hands, but they seemed to spell something out when held together. Chris cleared his throat and extended his right hand the length of the table toward Childress. He watched how, at first, Childress and Liz both began to react by letting go and stepping back, but then Childress gave Chris a puzzled look and extended his hand. As Chris grasped it and shook it hard, he unclenched his jaw long enough to utter, "I had forgotten you lost your dad that young. Thank you." Chris watched as Childress looked at Will with surprise, causing him to miss Chris' quick inspection of the tattoo on his hand, the one that read *Almas*.

Susan was stunned and almost gasped at what she saw. Before she heard her brother's kind words, she expected it was a ploy and that he would rip Childress' arm from his body. Instead, she saw a wave come across his face. She'd never seen it before and wasn't sure if she should question it or let this play out. She knew Childress and the woman with him were no good, but with a police detective seated with them, she felt confident guns would remain in holsters. She was confident but unsnapped her bag on the bench between her and the wall, making access to the compact pistol a bit easier, just in case. Then, she had to say something. She just had to.

"Chris, what's the matter? You look like you just saw a ghost." She watched as Chris withdrew his hand and adjusted his position in the booth, seated at an angle against the wall.

He turned to her, grinned, and shrugged his shoulders. *I intend to make him one soon.*

Susan used her foot to nudge her brother under the table and gave him a 'what's up' look. Then, her attention was taken by Liz, usually the talkative one of the two, who had something to say.

"Well, like Mark said. Sorry about your father."

Susan nodded and watched as the two clasped hands again and turned away. She watched Childress move quickly across the room, pushing through a group of old-timers chugging beers and trying to learn the two-step as a Brooks & Dunn tune played in the background.

⌇

With the exit now in sight, Childress's temper grew as his pace quickened, but Liz pulled back and spun him toward her.

"What the hell's the matter with you?" she asked.

"Mother fucker!"

"What?" she demanded. Childress grabbed her hand again and led her from the bar. Outside, stepping away from the few smokers coughing as they lit another one, Childress unloaded on her.

"You hired a shitty hitman is what. That bastard is still alive, and he knows something. He shook my hand. What the hell was that?" Childress turned away and stormed toward his BMW, with Liz racing after him.

❧

"Come on, let me up," Chris insisted as he pushed Bradshaw to move. The detective didn't budge and took another sip of his beer as he smiled across the table at Susan.

"Why?" Bradshaw asked half-jokingly.

"I need to wash my hands and get the shit off them," Chris said as he pushed at Bradshaw.

"Bullshit, hold it. I know that look. You're staying put until I hear that BMW race out of the parking lot. I don't know what the hell that just was, but something's up, and I'm keeping you from doing something stupid." Chris sat back in the booth, finished his beer, and slammed the bottle hard on the table. He stared across the table at Will.

"When we get home, we need to talk." Simultaneously, Susan and Bradshaw uttered the same comment as they shook their heads. "Uh oh."

After waving goodbye to Susan just past seven, Will and Chris entered their father's kitchen. Will nearly emptied a tube of Pringles before even looking at Chris. Neither had said a word since Chris led him into the room, spun a chair, and sat down. Finally, Chris spoke.

"So, are you ready?" he asked.

"Ready for what?" Will answered.

"Are you ready to tell me about the plane?"

CHAPTER NINE

Without saying a word, Chris left the room for a minute and returned with the hitman's laptop. He took a seat and began a search. He looked up at Will and then toward the kitchen's back door.

"Don't even think about it," Chris declared. Then, finally, he sat back in his chair.

"There you are, you little bastards."

A second later, he spun the old computer around so the screen faced his brother and pointed. Will let out a nervous cough and leaned in.

"So, what am I looking at?"

"Have you ever noticed the tattoos on Mark and Liz's hands?"

"Yeah, I went with them when they got them about a year ago. They wanted me to get some ink and offered to pay, but I told them you'd kill me if I did." Chris stared at Will.

"Interesting how they form a phrase when they put their hands together." Will nodded.

"Yeah, like a jigsaw puzzle."

"And what does it read when they do?"

"Almas Perdidas. It's Spanish for lost souls or some-thing like that. Why?" Chris got up from his chair and stood behind his brother. He leaned in close and pointed at something on the screen.

"Click on that icon. Click here," he directed. As Will followed orders, he looked up at Chris, who left his eyes on the screen.

"What the hell?"

"Now scroll down. Read the thread. It's signed off on with a capital L."

"They tried to have you killed. Really?"

"Yeah, but I'm still here, but the dipshit they sent after me isn't." Suddenly, Will jumped up from the table. He was in a panic. Chris had seen the behavior before and knew it was best to talk Will down with reassuring words and tone, which was the opposite of what he felt like doing. He watched as Will approached the door to escape, perhaps to run from the reality of what had just been revealed: that and all of its implications. Chris pulled a chair from the table and set it between the kitchen door and the hallway to the dining room. If Will were going to run for it, he'd have to get past his bigger, rougher older brother. With Will a cross-country running champion, a late-night foot pursuit across Bexar County was the last thing Chris was up for. What he was up for, though, were answers.

"Are you going to get in trouble for that? They could send you away, and what happens to me then?" Will asked. Chris shook his head no.

"No, everything will be fine as far as that goes. You

just can't discuss that with anyone, and I mean *anyone,* unless *I* say it's okay." Chris held out his right hand and extended his curled little finger.

"Come on, pinkie swear just like we have since we were kids." Chris watched as Will stared at the hand and let out a breath of relief as he watched the tension in his brother's face and body appear to calm. Then, Will bolted toward him. Chris jumped up, planning to block an escape move, but instead, he was nearly knocked over as Will wrapped his arms around him and held on tight. Chris did the same, but soon after began to tighten his bear hug grasp, just as he had since they were younger, until Will gave up and called out, "Uncle." Will stepped back and smiled at Chris, extending his hand and curled finger. "Pinkie swear."

"So the junkie in the parking lot. That's the guy they sent to hurt you?" Chris felt like his heart almost stopped as he struggled to maintain his composure.

"What?" How'd you know he was a junkie?" Chris watched as Will burst into laughter and pulled two Diet Coke's out of the refrigerator.

"Susan told me that's how your face got all scratched up. She said you told her some asshole jumped you, but you ran him off." Finally, Chris took a breath. *I sure did, and your two shithead friends are next.*

Chris took the soda and pulled his chair closer to the table.

"Okay, now sit down and click on that user name again. Scroll down until you find something about a B-17." He watches Will drink as he scrolls and sees his eyes grow large when he finds it and begins to read the details.

"So what do you think? How does that make you feel?" Chris asked.

Suddenly, Will stood up and threw his soda bottle across the room, smashing it against the dull white wooden cabinets. Chris nodded his approval.

"So I know how you feel, and so does that bottle. But tell me what you're feeling inside."

"Betrayed, I feel betrayed, okay?" Will shouted and then ran past him.

Chris sat quietly until he heard his brother's bedroom door slam closed and shook his head.

"I don't think so, little brother, not tonight."

After cleaning up the dishes in the sink, removing the trash, and changing into a black Eagles t-shirt and pair of gym shorts, Chris walked to Will's door and listened. Then he knocked and entered without asking. It had been a long time since Chris had been in there. He smiled at his brother seated on the floor against the wall and watched a gentle breeze move the white vertical blinds. He surveyed the room and smiled when he focused on the dozen framed photos on the wall at the foot of Will's bed before plopping down on the floor close to Will.

Chris pointed at a photo of him in his high school football uniform. Will smiled as he described the others.

"That's me, you, Susan, and Pop at Niagara Falls. Then we went to Rochester, where we rode on The Memphis Belle B-17, the movie one, and the Whiskey 7 C-47."

Chris rolled onto the floor and laughed when Will cringed at the cracking sounds coming from his brother's back.

"Ow!"

"Yeah, it gets tight sometimes, but that crack always does the trick." Chris sat up and pushed Will over. "Still a pushover, I see." Will sat up and shoved his brother back, pushing him over and saying, "Don't make me kick your ass." That went on for a few minutes, like brothers did all across the country, until Chris refocused on the photos.

"That was one hell of a trip," he began. "Probably the best, all things considered."

Will nodded.

"I think it did him some good. He wanted to show us where he took Mom for their honeymoon," Chris continued. "I saw the heartbreak in his eyes at the falls, but when we got him to the warbird show, I don't think he stopped smiling for a week." Chris got up and sat on the side of Will's bed.

"So now, tell me about the B-17 they stole. How were you involved, and where the hell is it?"

～

Will looked up at Chris and was amazed and confused. *These two assholes tried to have him killed, and he wants to talk about the airplane. I want him to focus on them and forget about the plane. I can't believe I fell for their lies. They conned me. Have they been lying to me all this time? Lying to me about everything? I know Liz doesn't care; she fakes it, but Mark? He's had my back since high school. He protected me when Chris wasn't here, which was a lot.* Will refocused on the photos on the wall and then back at his brother. He saw that familiar, impatient look starting to take hold – the same one Susan had perfected over the years.

"I want you to go after Mark and that bitch first," Will demanded.

~

Chris laughed and slid down on the floor, now at eye level with Will.

"Those two aren't going anywhere; they don't know I'm on to them. They don't know I have the laptop. I need to find that plane before anyone else does. If the police put it all together, you, little brother, might spend the next twenty years in jail. I don't think you'd like it there." Will sat quietly for a time. Chris knew how much to push him and when to let him be. He knew his brother would see the sense in the move, but he wanted him to agree to it first. Then, Chris began to feel the effects the hardwood floor was taking on his back and got up. He stood tall over Will and stared down at him.

"I need a beer and some Advil. I'll be in the living room if you need me."

He left Will alone with his thoughts and, after washing down the three brown-colored painkillers with a beer, he lowered himself slowly onto the sofa and stared across the coffee table at the worn blue recliner their father had sat in for so many years. Together, they'd sat and watched college and pro football games and every military-themed film ever made, including Band of Brothers, more times than he could remember. Finally, what he'd hoped for happened as he heard footsteps coming from the hall. He smiled as Will stopped in the entryway.

"I thought you might have fallen asleep," Chris said softly.

Will stepped closer and stood over him.

"So, what do you want to know?"

Chris smiled and grimaced as he forced himself up.

"Everything. And then you're going to have to tell Susan."

Will dropped his head as he groaned and plopped down beside his big brother.

CHAPTER TEN

SUSAN BOONE WAS accustomed to late-night dinners with coworkers, and tonight was no different. She and two young male staffers had parked at the bar in J. Alexanders in San Antonio and commiserated about their caseloads, love lives, and the fact that nobody seemed to have time for one. Federal prosecutors were known to be intelligent, relentless, and junkyard dogs when they sunk their teeth into a case, leaving little time for much else. The slight buzz she felt had helped dissolve the tension inside her, and she ordered a few appetizers for them to get at least some nourishment before it was time to call it a night. Then, she watched her phone dance on the bar.

"Ignore it," the staffer from upstate New York said.

"Well, at least you know it's not Norma," the other joked. Susan's glare almost burned a hole in the freshman attorney, who acknowledged he'd screwed up big time when he uttered the stupid joke.

"God, Susan. I'm sorry. I'm so sorry," he said with panic. She shook her head at him as she checked her phone and saw a text from Chris.

Can you come to Pop's tonight? We need to talk.

She shook her head and looked again at her staffers.

"Make sure he picks up the bill tonight!" she said and then responded to Chris.

Can't – dinner meeting.

Okay. How about in the morning?

Can't. I have court at nine.

Come early. Will has something important to tell you.

What????

Have the coffee ready. I'll be there at eight.

She slid the phone into her small, tan purse that hung from a gold hook under the bar and forced a smile just as the food arrived.

"It's always something.

Chris lay on his bed in the darkness. He couldn't sleep. His back was much better, but his mind and emotions were restless. He looked across at the digital clock and sighed when he saw 3:43 lit up in red. He sat up, turned on the light, and surveyed the room he grew up in. He thought of everything Will had confessed to earlier, more like divulged and needed to act. He'd take care of Childress and Liz in due time. They were hostiles, and he'd learned to handle those while the bullets flew overseas. As long as they didn't know he or Will were on to them, he figured he had time, maybe a week at best, to save his brother and hopefully something he thought of with reverence – the lost bird.

He looked at the posters he'd hung on the walls years before. The first was of Marines and the American flag on

Iwo Jima. He'd had the very rare honor of visiting that spot on Mount Suribachi, and it made him prouder to be a U.S. Marine more than anything. Then he turned his attention to a photo and quote from General Patton: "Give me an Army of West Point graduates, and I'll win a battle. Give me a handful of Texas Aggies, and I'll win a war." He stood up and stretched for a minute, approached another motivational poster, and this one was all he needed. It was a quote from President Ronald Reagan that read, "Some people wonder all their lives if they've made a difference. The Marines don't have that problem." That was it. He walked to the kitchen and loaded the old Mr. Coffee his parents had used for longer than he could remember. He crept down the hall, listened at Will's door, and was pleased to hear nothing coming from his room. Ten minutes later, he walked past Will's door, a camo backpack slung over his shoulder and a camo gear bag filled with binoculars, night vision goggles, a plate carrier that civilians might call a bulletproof vest, an assault rifle, and enough ammunition to fight a small war. He filled a thermos with coffee, grabbed the three bananas from a bowl on the counter, and left.

He climbed behind the wheel after checking the oil and fluid levels under the hood. The dome light lit up the interior as he looked over his shoulder and recalled his days in Iraq; his desert camo gear spread from door to door. As the engine idled, Chris typed the destination into his phone. San Antonio to Lake Havasu City, Arizona, was 1173 miles to the west, and he fully intended to be where the B-17 was last seen, according to Will, when the sun broke the horizon the next morning.

In Texas, Susan pulled up to the Boone family home right on time at 8 a.m. It was early; the pot of coffee she'd ingested was just kicking in, and she needed to find out what was up and then get to court. Federal Judges were big on punctuality, and she'd never been late and didn't intend to be this morning. She reached over the front seat console of her pickup and grabbed the brown bag of hot breakfast tacos she knew her brothers would soon be fighting over. She didn't see Chris' pickup in the drive, which wasn't unusual. For years, it could turn up there, around back, or down the road, depending on how much fun he'd had the night before. Once inside, she called out but didn't hear a sound. She looked at the Mr. Coffee on the counter and then felt it - *cold*.

"Chris? Will? Where is everybody?"

She dropped the bag on the table and headed down the hallway. She stopped at her father's door and cried when she thought of the loving father she'd never see there again. But she fought back her emotion and then moved to Will's room. Not there.

"Guys? Where the heck are you? I don't have time for games this morning."

She stood for a moment and listened. As kids, her brothers had jumped out and scared her way too many times for her to forget. *They're hiding in here, damn it. Come on, guys. I can't today,* she thought. She shrugged her shoulders and walked to Chris' door.

"Well, that's a first," she declared. "A Marine never leaves his bed unmade." She returned to the kitchen, surveyed the room, and looked outside for Chris' truck.

"Damn it, Chris!"

Just as she pulled her phone from her suit dark blue

slacks to call him, it rang. When she read the caller ID, she was livid.

"So, how much trouble is he in?" Chris asked.

"What? Who? Where the heck are you two?"

⤚

Behind the wheel, westbound on I-10 approaching Fort Stockton, Chris wasn't sure he heard his sister correctly.

"What do you mean, where are you two? I'm on my way to Arizona, and Will's there with you." When Chris heard his sister's response, it felt like the world had stopped turning.

"He's not with you?"

"No, there's no sign of either one of you. What the hell's going on?" she demanded.

"Childress and his girlfriend tried to have me killed. They were the two behind the B-17 that was stolen, and they suckered Will into it. He's supposed to be there waiting for you. He's supposed to tell you everything."

⤚

Susan ran back into Will's bedroom and checked his closet. His backpack was still there.

"I don't think he's run away. His stuff's still here. Damn it, Chris, why didn't you tell me this last night?" Then, Susan saw a phone on the night table, but she knew he never went anywhere without it.

"Chris, his phone's here. I'm going to call the police."

"No, don't. Give me some time to think."

"He helped steal the plane and those bastards – that junkie the other night. Did they send him to kill you?"

"Yep. Now, I want you to take a few breaths and look under the cushion on Pop's recliner. There's a laptop, the hitman's laptop. It has everything you need to see to prove it was them. The password's Cowboys."

"Where's the hitman?" she asked.

"No comment," he replied.

"But what about Will? Do you think they have him? Do you think they know? Oh God, Chris, he wouldn't have called them and told them what he knows, would he? They'd have come here for sure and taken him if he did. He could be dead right now."

"Breathe. We'll figure this out."

"I'm going to call the police."

"No, don't. Not yet. Check out the laptop, and then maybe we can bring Billy into this. But we can't let Will get jailed, not even for a day. He wouldn't last in there. We have to protect him, no matter what."

Susan ended the call, picked up the brown bag, and threw it against the window over the kitchen sink. Suddenly, she heard someone standing behind her. She tensed. *Was it them?*

CHAPTER ELEVEN

IN THE KITCHEN, happy he'd scared her again, Will wrapped his arms around Susan and lifted her off the ground. She struggled until he put her down. When she turned, she was overjoyed and furious at the same time, but Will didn't see her face. He was focused on the food.

"What the hell you do that for?"

"God, you're all wet." She looked down at her white blouse and yelled at him.

"You got *me* all wet! Christ, Will. Where the hell have you been?"

Will laughed as he passed her and began to pick at the remnants of what had been once hot tacos.

"I went for a long run."

"Without your phone?" she shouted, holding it up. Will shook his head.

"No, that's Pop's. I like to look at all of his pictures," he said as he walked to the refrigerator and began chugging from an orange juice container. As he did, he pointed to the phone he'd just set on the counter as he snuck in.

"I don't have time for this shit today, mister. Throw

some clothes on and meet me in the car." Will shook his head no.

"I need to get a shower."

"Bring a towel, but you've got five minutes. Chris said you've got a few things to tell me, and you can do it in the car!" Will didn't move.

"Okay, I'll just call the police." Will shoved the container inside the refrigerator and ran past her toward his room. She shook her head, watched him disappear down the hallway, and then went into the living room, where she recovered the laptop Chris had told her to grab. She checked her watch and then walked to her car. Once there, she called Chris, but to her surprise, he didn't answer. She sent a text.

Found our cross-country runner/brother. I have the laptop. Headed to court.

Susan studied her brother in the car as she sped through the morning rush hour traffic.

"You okay over there?"

Will didn't respond. She looked across at him again and poked his shoulder. As he turned, she saw the tears in his eyes and then watched as he wiped them away with the sleeves of his black Spurs t-shirt. Then, she saw his look of apparent sorrow turn.

"You know, while you and Chris were away in college and the Marines, Mark was always there for me while you two weren't," he began. She wanted to respond but saw he wasn't finished. "I get it. You were doing what you wanted to do. I'm not blaming anybody. But Mark was always there, except when he joined the Army. And then he came home, with Liz latched to him, and things between us picked up where they left off."

"You remember he joined the Army but was kicked out with a dishonorable discharge, right? That's why he came back so soon." She watched his face, hoping her brother would finally realize for himself what his so-called friend actually was.

"Yeah, he said some guy tried to steal his stuff in the barracks. They got into a fight, and that got him kicked out of the Army." Susan swerved to avoid a big rig that had just blown a trailer tire and turned the highway into a game of bumping cars. She caught her breath as Will turned in his seat to watch the mayhem unfold behind them.

"Will, he wasn't telling you the truth about that either." Will turned to face forward.

"Will, he was caught stealing from another soldier's gear. They fought; he pulled a knife and stabbed the guy. He beat the charges on a technicality, but they kicked him out, plain and simple. You can look it up on the internet if you want. It's there for everyone to see."

༈

In Arizona, Pat Monahan's morning had been much less exciting than what was taking place in Texas; He'd been able to find a quiet place to stay in Lake Havasu, somewhat off the beaten path. At the hotel he'd stayed in near Parker the day before, two HVAC contractors had recognized him in the parking lot and gotten in his face. Luckily, the hotel clerk had seen the confrontation escalate and called the police. He was relieved when the officer had given them the choice of returning to work or dealing with the K-9 in the rear seat of his black and white Ford

SUV. But as the two walked away, cursing at him as they walked away, he was surprised by the officer's remark after he thanked him for his help.

"Do me a favor. Get the heck out of Parker. You can't give up a warbird without a fight and expect to get any sort of a welcome here."

Now, at the Nautical Inn, Pat could sit quietly on a picnic table and watch as streams of orange and yellow painted the sky as the sun set. He was growing more frustrated as the days passed, fed by stories on the local news. One he saw was an interview with his co-pilot and former friend Charlie Taylor and his wife Liz, who both questioned his effort, or lack of it, during the theft. Then another troubled him more when a state official related, "Our assets are stretched thin already chasing drug traffickers and illegal immigrants, and there is nothing left to spend on finding an old airplane." But Pat was okay with that. He was on the hunt and determined to find the plane or at least some answers as to where she'd been taken if it was the last thing he did. With nobody waiting for him back in Palm Springs, this was the only thing he wanted – and needed, to do.

Sipping a mug of freshly brewed coffee, he'd retaken his seat on the table and faced the lake in anticipation of another light show, a morning one growing from the east. He'd stopped shaving, hoping a bit of a gray beard might serve as a disguise, and he'd abandoned his well-worn blue Air Force ball cap, instead wearing a white NASCAR one Linda had stuffed in his Christmas stocking months before. In town, he'd driven across the famous London Bridge that had been brought there from England and reassembled, but now it was time to pick up where he'd left off and find another national treasure, the one he'd lost.

❧

Outside the courtroom in San Antonio, Will sat quietly, playing games on his phone, and followed his sister's instructions not to move or talk to anyone. He kept his head down, locked on his screen. Then, he heard a crowd of people exiting from across the hallway and looked up to see Susan storming toward him.

"Come on, let's go," she snapped without stopping. Will jumped up and fast-walked to catch up to her, and just as he got beside her, she got a call.

"It's Chris!" She kept walking, giving polite smiles or frowns to defense attorneys and others she'd done battle with in court.

"Where the hell have you been? I called and texted you, but then I had to go into court."

"I got your message. Strangest thing. No cell service for at least thirty miles. So he's okay?"

"Yes, he's with me."

"And where's that?"

"The courthouse, where else?"

"What?!?" Chris yelled.

❧

From inside his pickup, spent paper coffee cups, food, and candy bar wrappers were thrown in a pile on the passenger side's floor; Chris was beside himself.

"You took him out in public to a place where criminals, snitches, and all sorts of characters walk around?" He listened, trying to calm himself down, and from the delay before his sister responded, he was expecting to get a bit of what he'd given.

"Listen, I had a case that I couldn't be late for. The judge is a real ballbuster. But I'm not the one who decided to drive to Arizona overnight. You do know they have these things called airplanes?"

Chris looked at the speedometer and thought the "80" he'd set the cruise control to was enough to keep up with the dozens of semis flying across the interstate. He waited, knowing Susan was frustrated.

"Susan, I'm sorry. But you need to stop thinking like a prosecutor and start acting like a bodyguard until you have him hidden away somewhere. If you can, get him out of there. Make sure you're not followed. They taught you how to do that. Take him to a hotel, pay cash, and use an alias," Chris insisted. "Did he tell you the story yet?"

"Some. I was going to dive into the laptop next since I lost the case and have the rest of the day freed up."

Chris nodded as he adjusted the rearview mirror to get the blinding morning sun out of his eyes.

"Okay. But please hide him and yourself somewhere. The people who had the plane stolen had money and power, and connections usually go hand in hand with that. We don't know who's behind this, but we have to keep him safe," Chris said, his voice trailing off.

"We promised Pop, and besides that, I kind of like the knucklehead."

✍

Will knew the way to Susan's office, but suddenly, she turned left instead of the right as she ended the call with their brother. He slowed.

"Keep walking. Go to my car in the parking lot and wait there. I have to get a few things from my office, and I'll meet you there in five minutes," she said.

"Why? What's going on? Is Chris okay?"

"He's fine, and I'll explain everything once we're in the car. Now go!" she said as she pointed toward the garage parking sign. She stepped to the side to escape the pedestrian traffic and watched until she saw Will disappear through the doors. Then, she headed to her office, informing her staff that she wasn't feeling well and would take a few days off. She slid the laptop Chris had acquired into her already full briefcase and then stopped. She stared at the drawers of her desk, opened the middle one on the left, removed a black 9mm semi-automatic pistol, and dropped it into her dark blue suit jacket pocket. She stared at the bulge it made.

"Shit," she declared, removing half of the files from her briefcase and sliding the gun inside. She smiled.

"Better." Then, without saying another word, she left the office and disappeared into the flow of people navigating the hallway.

Their room at the Embassy Suites on the north side of town overlooked the San Antonio airport, and Susan paused her study of the laptop to watch Will as he studied everything aviation he could see from the large window. She knew he loved airplanes and was pleased she'd chosen the right place to stay. She resumed her tour of the dark web and was stunned at the goings on she found there. As a Federal prosecutor, she felt like a kid in a dark candy store and wanted to get to work, but first, she needed to focus on her brothers and their safety. When a knock at the door startled them both, she gestured for Will to be quiet and stay put as she approached the door, her gun held close to her chest. Rather than look through the peephole, she stood close to the wall and called out.

"Who is it?" she asked.

"Housekeeping," a strange-sounding voice responded.

"Don't need any," she said.

"It's me, Susan. It's Billy."

She turned and smiled at Will as she drew back the latch, flipped the deadbolt, and slid her pistol under the seat cushion of the green and black fabric chair near the door. Once Billy was inside, she redid the locks and gestured for him to sit. Instead, their family friend put that role aside and presented himself as an officer of the law.

"So what's with all the secrecy? What are we doing here at a damn hotel?"

"You ready?" she asked, cocking her head.

"Yes. Now, let's get to it. What's up?" Billy looked across at Will, who remained consumed with the views of the airport.

"Hey Will, you doing alright?" Will turned quickly.

"Hey Billy," he responded without taking his eyes off the planes.

Bradshaw returned his focus to Susan and held his hands up, questioning.

"Okay, here goes. Someone tried to kill Chris, and

there's a good chance they're after Will." Billy's jaw and his hands dropped like rocks.

"Short version. Mark Childress ordered a hit on Chris after the confrontation you broke up at the bar the other night."

"No way."

"Yep. Some asshole attacked Chris in the parking lot there the next night. Chris got the best of him and forced him to talk. Liz connected with the dipshit on the dark web and set it up. He forced the guy to show him the dark web stuff on his laptop, and then the guy attacked Chris again, and he had to kill him in self-defense." Susan watched as Billy walked to the window and stood alongside Will.

"You sound like his lawyer."

"I am," she said as she walked to the window. She stood behind Will and placed her hands on her brother's shoulders. Susan knew Billy had a choice; he could be a friend or do his duty and be a cop. Finally, he spoke.

"Where'd this happen – the self-defense and all?" Susan knew he'd made his choice and patted Will's shoulders.

"South of here." Billy turned away and began pacing the room.

"And this is all factual? No twisting or omitting details? We are talking about Chris, you know," he stated, his tone sounding more like a detective. Susan let out a slight laugh.

"Yes, we're talking about Chris, and yes, it's gospel."

She looked down at her right hand, her fingers crossed. Billy walked back to his spot alongside them at the window.

"There was a trailer fire down in Elmendorf. They found remains in it. Somebody who lived near there said they heard a gunshot. They figured someone was shooting at a dog or something, if I remember the news story right. They said right after that, they saw the whole thing go up in a blaze and called the fire department."

≈

Billy walked to the credenza, popped a K-cup into the black Keurig, and stared at the machine until it began to hiss and spew hot caffeine into one of the hotel's black ceramic mugs.

Chris. One of these days, this shit will catch up to you, and my badge or your sister's won't be able to keep you out of jail.

He sipped at the coffee as he walked to the window and focused on Susan's face.

"So where's the laptop?"

≈

"Locked up in my safe."

"You see this as a federal case all of a sudden?"

"Not the hit on Chris, but there was evidence of a crime that falls under my purview, which I need to pursue."

"Really?"

"Yep. That B-17 that was stolen. That laptop has evidence that can help us track who took it and who funded the deal. It indicates they took it across state lines." Susan felt confident she'd made her case. Having just put her brother's lives and her career on the line, she prayed this family friend would believe her and do what she needed next.

"Okay, so what can I do? What do you need from

me?" Billy asked. Inside, Susan did cartwheels, but her expression remained stoic.

"BOLOs and arrest warrants on Mark Childress and Liz Tyler for conspiracy to commit murder," she stated. She watched Bradshaw. His expression indicated that her ask seemed reasonable, but then it changed as he focused on Will.

"Hey, Will. We've known each other for a long time. Have you ever lied to me?"

Will seemed surprised at the question, which made Susan smile. She'd been trained to push people in interviews and under oath on the stand. She knew how to read people and knew Billy did, too. Will's reaction was perfect. *Now, if he can just stick the landing.*

"No, sir. Never have." Susan and Billy smiled at his response as she let out a silent, calming breath.

"Good. Did you know anything about the hit they put out on Chris?"

Will laughed at first, but Susan watched, as did the detective, as anger took over his face.

"No, sir. I'd have called you or told Susan or Chris if I had heard anything about it. I'm not stupid. Those two are evil, lying, back-stabbing bastards, and I hope they get whatever you or Chris can do to them." Susan smiled at her brother and watched as Billy nodded and smiled.

"Thought so, but I had to ask. It's my job," he told them and then focused on Susan.

"Do you want me to put a few uniforms on the door until we round them up?"

Susan shook her head no.

"No, but thanks, Billy. I'm going to take him up to

Pop's place on the lake once it's dark. We'll stay out of sight there until you tell me the coast is clear."

Suddenly, Susan felt Will's shoulders tense.

"But-"

She pushed on his shoulder as she spoke.

"But nothing young man. And not another word out of you. We all told you about those two!" She hoped Will was smart enough to follow her lead, or perhaps the words she'd chosen to chastise him would quiet him until Billy left the room. She smiled at Billy, walking past him, hoping he'd follow her to the door. He did but abruptly pushed it closed just as she opened it for him. She turned to him with surprise.

"One question. Why is Chris in Arizona? Why didn't he just run up to the lake if he's laying low? Only a few of us know about your pop's place." Susan had an answer ready that she knew Billy would believe, especially since it was the truth.

"You know Chris," she said, shrugging her shoulders as she smiled and shook her head.

He laughed as he let himself out. Then Susan threw the locks and watched through the peephole until she saw him disappear from view. She turned to Will.

"Okay, let's get packed up. We've got a plane to catch." Will looked at her with surprise.

"We're flying to Johnson City? It's only like sixty miles." Susan smiled.

"No, we're headed to Palm Springs. There's an FBI agent there that might want to help."

CHAPTER TWELVE

IN A REMOTE part of Arizona, Chris had pulled off Highway 95 and stopped west of where Will said the B-17 had been taken. To the rare vehicle that drove by, Chris had staged his pickup and gear to look as though he was simply a hiker, a wanderer, enjoying the desolation and solitude. After studying every map of the area available and not finding any mention of an aircraft runway in the grid, he planned a one-hour reconnaissance hike and then another hour back to his truck just as he lost daylight, so he set off. He'd made a reservation at a hotel in nearby Lake Havasu and had a date with a king-size bed, but that depended, of course, on if he made it back. But there was just one problem: he hated snakes. As far back as grade school, while many of his friends learned how to deal with them in rural South Texas, Chris would always be tense and tried his best to continue. Then, as they got older, while many hunted for rattlesnakes to take to the rattlesnake roundup events, he avoided those excursions and instead focused elsewhere by watching football videos. Then, shipped overseas to Iraq in uniform, his fellow Marines quickly donned Chris with the nickname "Indy" after Indiana Jones, the fictional character who also hated snakes. Chris checked his watch. It was time to get moving, or he'd lose daylight on his trek back to the pickup. He double-checked his gear, opting to leave his plate carrier and four full magazines behind, and threw a small desert camo backpack over his shoulder. Then he headed out.

Finally, he'd arrived. He knelt in the gritty, sandy soil and crawled to the crest of the hill. He was thrilled he hadn't come up on any snakes as he walked there, but now, lying at ground level, he felt most vulnerable as his heart began to race. He took a few calming deep breaths, pictured his brother Will standing dressed in an orange jumpsuit behind bars, and began to move. As he peeked over the top, there it was, just as his brother had described it to him: a sand-blown black asphalt runway, a large Quonset hut painted in tan and brown camouflage, its tall sliding front doors open perhaps a foot, and nothing more. He pulled a monocular from his pack, wiped the sweat from his eyes, and began to scan the area, looking for anything that could be a threat. With the sun now behind him, he studied the shadows. Then he slid down and maintained some distance, eventually crossing a dirt road that snaked between two hills and led to the building. He climbed to a vantage point with a view of the opposite side of the building, the rear, where Will had said he and Liz had picked up Mark and his pilots after they delivered the B-17.

"Make-A-Wish my ass," Chris whispered. "Little brother, they played you like a fiddle."

He watched for snakes near his path and bad guys near the building, but there were none. He sat for a moment, scanning the ground around him as he drank an orange sports drink, and then, it was time to move in. As he stood up, he patted the holstered gun on his right thigh and stored the monocular, pulling an assault rifle with a collapsible stock from his pack as he began to cover the fifty yards between him and the structure. When he reached the building, he stood in the shadow and felt the temperature change as his eyes began to adjust. He stared at the vehicle tracks, mostly blown over but still there. He shook his head, wishing Will was there with him so he could kick his butt. Hooking his shades into his shoulder strap, he put his hand on the door, took another deep breath, and crept inside, ready for anything. But then his heart sank. She was gone.

Chris scanned the edges of the building's interior as he recognized the familiar aromas of the hydraulic fluid, oil, and fuel that stained the concrete floor. He walked to a line of black drums and kicked at the first one, the sound amplified inside the cavernous space. Empty. Will's story continued to check out. The beautiful warbird had been fed here, but where she was now was anybody's guess. He stepped to the slight opening between the hangar doors and squinted in the fading sunlight. Donning his gold mirror shades and keeping his weapon ready, he slid through the opening and stood momentarily, hoping to see anything that might help give him something to work. Then, shaking his head in defeat, he began walking toward the sun, his truck, and some much-needed rest. An hour later, he was back at his truck, relieved, as he stowed his gear and took a leak while guzzling a liter of cold water. Then, back in the pickup, he headed north on SR95 toward Havasu. He tried to call Susan and Will, but with no signal, he dropped the phone in a cuprest and turned on Sirius. He didn't search for news, though; he needed tunes to get him the rest of the way and turned up the volume as his favorite Tim McGraw songs began to play. Twenty minutes later, the flashing red and blue lights of the Arizona Highway Patrol ahead of him caused him to check the speedometer, which read seventy-six, and ease off the gas.

Slowing as he approached the vehicles on the shoulder to the northbound side, he killed the music and focused on a uniformed female trooper standing with a man and a woman wearing white golf shirts and khakis, standing maybe thirty feet in. He passed an unmarked white Dodge Charger sedan with California plates and then a second vehicle, a silver and black SUV with a light bar on the roof. But he needed to refocus on the road ahead as a gasoline tanker roared toward him in the southbound lane.

Jones and Simms had spent much of the day staring at maps of Arizona as they made their way to the crime scene near Havasu. Simms had pushed Jones to drive faster and get there before they lost the light, but Jones wasn't taking suggestions from his younger female partner. He outranked her and never let her forget it. He never said it out loud; his demeanor and lack of interest in anything she had to offer said it all. After introductions and handshakes, the trooper led them to the crime scene and pointed to three burned areas on the ground.

"Coroner says all three were shot, single nine-millimeter hollow points to the head. Whoever did this set the bodies on fire afterward. She pointed to a dirt road. "Forensics says it was a full-size SUV," the trooper suggested. Jones smirked as he followed her lead. *Don't need a degree to figure that out.* The three stopped as Simms shook her head.

"So they're thinking the vehicle turned onto the road, pulled off it, shot the three, and then drove away?" The trooper nodded as her attention shifted to a red Kenworth tractor pulling a gasoline tanker trailer sped by. She shook her head at him as the driver tapped his air horn.

"That's one lucky son of a bitch," she said. "If I were running radar, I'd have had him for sure." Jones and Simms kept focus on the ground, but both nodded. Simms shook her head.

"Any shells?"

"Nope. They swept the area, but they did find something. Whoever did this cleaned up after themselves, but he or they missed something. Forensics found an empty beer bottle in the sand, and it's in Phoenix at the crime lab." Jones smirked again, which drew an eye roll from Simms that wasn't lost on the trooper.

"Hell, there's probably a thousand beer bottles tossed every week along this stretch."

The trooper stepped to Jones and stopped close.

"True, but it was a bottle of Lone Star. We don't see it all that much out here. It's a Texas brand." Jones shook his head and began to speak, but she cut him off.

"But we found a bottle of Lone Star under one of the bodies. They probably fell on it when they were shot.

Whoever cleaned this up missed both bottles, and if we can pull a print off either, well, you're a big city detective. You know how it works from there." Simms giggled, which drew a glare from her partner.

"So my bet is the shooter pulled off the road so everyone could take a leak, and as they did, he popped them," Simms suggested. Jones nodded and surveyed the area as Simms and the trooper smiled.

"About an hour before you arrived, the lab got an ID from the bottle under dead guy number two. The guy's from Michigan. In his late fifties, he had a criminal record and used to have a pilot's license. Flew cargo planes in and out of Central America after he got kicked out of the Air Force." Simms's eyes grew wide, and then she looked to see Jones kicking at the ground.

"You thinking what I'm thinking?" she whispered to the trooper, who nodded.

"Somebody steals a B-17, and then we find a dead pilot, a bad guy, and his buddies near the side of the road," the trooper said as she watched another big rig fly by on the highway.

"How soon before we get a match on the second bottle?"

"Soon, I hope. Give me *your* card, and I'll forward the reports as they come in if that's okay." Jones stepped close.

"I wonder if this has anything to do with that old plane that was stolen."

The trooper bit her lip, and Simms watched the woman tense with frustration.

"That *old plane* is a piece of American history, mister. It flew during World War II and helped beat those Nazi bastards. Unfortunately, only a few of them are still flying, and yes, I think these three had something to do with stealing it. This is a big state, and whoever did this was smart, but now we've got something to work with. We'll find her and who did this. I'm very sure of that. We might not have had every resource looking for her because we're stretched thin, but now that people have been killed, they'll put more assets on it." She stared at Jones.

"I think you've worn out your welcome here, detective. It's time for you to get in your car and head back to Palm Springs. The resources of the Arizona Highway Patrol will take it from here." Simms watched as Jones mumbled something, turned, and walked toward their car. She handed the trooper her card and then shook her hand.

"My emails' on there. Thanks for the help, and if you're ever in Palm Springs, call me. I'd like to buy you a beer." Simms turned to see Jones get into the passenger side of their vehicle.

"Now I'll get a rendition of his silent treatment, a lecture, and then maybe some lactose intolerance if I know that asshole." Both women laughed.

"Well, you could always shoot him and dump him out here. Happens all the time," the trooper said as she looked past Simms and saw Jones staring at them. Simms shook her head.

"Worst I could do, maybe, was accidentally tase him."

"Safe travels," the trooper said as she read the card. "Detective Simms."

⏃

In Floresville, Texas, Billy Bradshaw walks into a dive bar and stands near the door, surveying the few patrons who conveniently turn away in their chairs and look at the exit sign across the room, the door under it still closed. Satisfied the threat level seemed to be pretty low, he approached the bartender, a tall, thin man in his thirties with a lean build covered with ink.

"You seen Mark and Liz in here this week?" he asked, but the bartender ignored him and kept toweling the bar top. Bradshaw scanned the room again, all eyes anywhere but on him.

Then, in the blink of an eye, he cracked the bartender hard on the side of the head, sending the man to the floor. He looked at the patrons, back at the entrance, and walked behind the bar.

He reached down and pulled the man up by the ears.

"Hear me now, you dumb son of a bitch?"

Dazed and confused, the bartender put up his hands in surrender as Bradshaw let go.

"No, I haven't seen them in here today. Why?"

"None of your fucking business. If they come in, tell them I'm looking for them. We need to talk. And don't ever ignore me again. I kept you out of jail so you could take care of your mother, but that came with conditions, remember?"

As Bradshaw walked from behind the bar, a patron who had returned from having a smoke out back stood in his way, glaring. He was much bigger than the detective or the man lying on the dirty, wet floor. The scars across the man's face and bald head and the cold stare in his eyes told Bradshaw he'd probably been in fights all his life. The two locked eyes until Bradshaw pulled back his dark blue suit coat to reveal a shiny silver detective's badge and a holstered black handgun.

"He must have slipped. It's really wet back there," Bradshaw stated and then waited, watching the man in his way plot, his eyes now working through his options.

"Should I take this jacket off, or are you going to get out of my way?" he asked in a firm, confident tone.

He watched the man study the patrons, who had turned back to see whatever was unfolding at the bar. When he saw two men, perhaps in their late fifties and seated in a back corner, shake their heads no, he relented and moved out of the way. Bradshaw had followed the man's eyes and smiled when he recognized the two off-duty policemen. They exchanged nods, and then Bradshaw left the bar, pushing past the roadblock without issue.

Outside, Bradshaw leaned against the front fender of his black Dodge Charger sedan and surveyed the parking lot, shaking his head.

"Well, that'll force those two rats to run," he whispered. "I just hope you tossed that gun in a lake somewhere, Chris."

꿍

Westbound on I-10 and glad the setting sun had finally lost its light, inside the black late model BMW Childress had driven for years, he checked his rearview mirror and then the speedometer on the dash. Riding shotgun as she always did, Liz checked her side view mirror and then read their speed out loud.

"Ninety-two," she said as she sat forward and turned

down the radio. "If I have to listen to another Lynyrd Skynyrd song, I'm getting out, even at ninety-two," she complained.

"Come on, Mark, don't you think you should slow down just a bit? Bad enough, the cops are looking for us, but if we get pulled over for speeding." She grew more frustrated as Childress shook his head no.

"Everybody's speeding. Look, I switched plates back at that truck stop, and we're just blending in with the traffic." She studied him for a minute and watched as her silence caused him to look over.

"Are you sure we're doing the right thing? Shouldn't we just bail and head for the border? We've got enough money to last a long time."

"No way. She owes us money. Even if that old dude isn't dead yet, I want the rest of the money, and then, maybe, we can drive straight to Mexico."

Liz shook her head in disagreement as she stared at the headlights headed east.

"We could go to Vegas. It's right up the road from there." She watched him smile.

"You know, we could blend in well there. She nodded in agreement and then turned the radio up just a bit.

"And all we'd need is another lonely kid with a sad face," she whispered.

CHAPTER THIRTEEN

CHRIS PASSED UNDER a few palm trees at the Nautical Inn as he carried his gear to his room. After being in the barren Arizona countryside's dust, sand, and silt, his SOP would have been to break everything down, clean and inspect the weapons, and have them ready to roll, but that would have to wait until morning. The cold shower had cleaned him up, but he needed a beer and a good steak before calling it a night. He'd run for days without sleep in Iraq, so this little adventure was relatively easy on him. Now seated happily at the bar, he scrolled through his phone as he glanced up at the ballgame on the TV, nursing his beer and waiting for dinner to arrive. Then, he saw a familiar face from the news, and the man saw him, too. Chris studied him for a moment, giving a slight smile.

Seated at the far end of the bar and away from the TV, Pat Monahan had endured another frustrating, fruitless day but had enjoyed his meal and coffee. That was until another stranger gave him the eye. Pat focused on the ballgame as he dropped two twenties on the bar. He watched the stranger regard the server as the man's dinner arrived and slid out the side entrance into the night without incident.

❧

Thousands of feet somewhere over New Mexico, Susan Boone and her brother Will sat quietly in the small commuter jet. They waited for the flight attendant to finish serving their drinks before continuing their discussion. As Susan fought to open a little blue bag of mini pretzels, Will laughed as he grabbed it and opened it for her.

"Tell me again why you lied to Billy," he whispered as the cabin lights were dimmed.

"It's just how we work. Keep what you're up to close and only share with people who need to know." Will studied her.

"But it makes it look like you don't trust him."

Will turned away and stared at the window. Having just lost their father, betrayed by who he thought of as his best friend, and now his sister – an attorney – lying to a cop, a family friend, this was all too much for him to process. Then, he felt Susan's hand rest on his forearm.

"Sometimes in my world, it's best not to trust anyone. Look at what your so-called friends got you into and tried to do to Chris. Billy's a family friend to us and a close friend to Chris, but we don't know who we can trust right now, so it's better to be safe than sorry, right?"

Will didn't answer. Her words had just pressed the dagger in a little deeper, and this wound to his heart was still fresh. Without saying another word, Will needed to check out. He closed his eyes and hoped sleep would take him from this nightmare.

The sunrise had made it a perfect morning for Pat Monahan. Sitting on the picnic table at the lake's edge, he sipped his coffee and soaked it all in. But then, he heard someone walking up behind him. He shook his head, disappointed that someone had the nerve to disturb his tranquility. As he turned, he tensed. The man who had eyeballed him in the bar the night before stood staring at him. It was clear to Pat that his person was probably ex-military or perhaps a wannabe who liked to dress in desert camo and act the part. Maybe the guy wanted to call him a coward or worse. Then he noticed the stranger was holding a coffee in each hand. *Oh great. Another reporter trying to befriend me to get a story.*

Pat stood up and looked past the stranger. His Jeep was close by, and so were his weapons, but then he realized his chances of making it there were slim at seventy years old and with this big guy in his way. He watched as the man turned, looked back at the Jeep, and laughed.

"I'm not a threat, Pat. I brought you some coffee," the man said as he walked to the table, set a cup on it, and then took a few steps back.

"Look, I don't want any trouble. I just want to be left alone," Pat told the stranger, then watched in disbelief as he stepped forward and sat down.

∽

"I recognized you in the bar last night," Chris said. "My name's Chris Boone, and we're here doing the same thing." He watched as Pat took another look at his Jeep.

"Oh yeah, what's that?" Pat asked.

"Trying to find her." Chris studied Pat. He could see the tension in the face of a once proud Air Force pilot now blamed for surrendering a national treasure. Then, as the man spoke, Chris watched the man's shoulders drop.

"I didn't have anything to do with the hijacking. They could have shot us and crashed the plane if I had tried anything."

Based on the interviews Chris had watched on TV, he believed him and gestured for Pat to sit. Pleased that he did, it was time to share what he knew.

"I know where they took her," Chris said and grinned when he saw a hint of life creep back into the pilot's expression.

"And how would you know that?"

"Because they drug my little brother into it. He told me where they took her, and I'm going to do everything I can to find her and kick their asses." Chris knocked the lid off his coffee and took a long draw. Then another as he studied Pat.

"Want to help or keep looking for her on your own?"

Chris stood up and extended his hand across the table. He watched as Pat studied him for a moment; he could see the wheels running in his head and was relieved when Pat finally took it.

Finishing his coffee, Chris pointed to his dusty old Toyota pickup truck across the parking lot.

"That's my ride. I've got all sorts of gear on board. All sorts. Just in case."

Pat reached down, picked up his coffee, and drank it without stopping.

"Army or Marines?"

"Semper Fi," Chris said with pride.

As the men began to walk toward the parking lot, they continued their conversation.

"What's that you jarheads say? Improvise, adapt, overcome?"

Chris laughed as he shook his head. He hadn't been called a jarhead in a long time.

"You got it right. Now, are you ready to go, or does an old airman like you need to take a dump or something? We're wasting time otherwise."

"Old my ass," Pat said as they walked.

"That's the spirit."

As the two approached the front of Chris' pickup, he watched as Pat began to veer off.

"Seriously? Can't you hold it? There's plenty of spots out in the desert to take a leak."

Chris raised the hood on his truck and began to check the fluid levels but then stopped when he saw Pat open the door to his Jeep. Once he saw Pat was retrieving a small black gear bag, he refocused on the fluids until he heard Pat say, "Cheese." When he looked up, Pat took his picture and then made a request.

"Let me see your ID."

"Seriously?" Chris asked as he reached into his pocket and withdrew a money clip. He picked through the cards until he held up his Armed Forces ID card.

"Twenty-year man, I'm impressed," Pat said.

After Pat took the photo, Chris slid the clip back into his pocket, closed the hood, and got behind the wheel. He watched and shook his head as Pat took a picture of the truck's front license plate.

"Burnin' daylight,' Chris called out from his open driver's side window.

"Better to be safe than sorry," Pat responded as he sat in the passenger seat and put on his seat belt.

Chris started the truck and looked over at his new partner.

"You ready?"

"Sure am."

"What are you going to do with the photos you took?" Chris asked as he put the truck in gear and drove out of the hotel parking lot.

"In case I wind up dead in the desert, I want my sister to know who did it. She's with the FBI." As Chris raced over a speed mound in the road, he laughed.

"That'll only help if you send them to her," Chris said as he watched Pat realize he hadn't yet. Pat shook his head, expressing his frustration.

"Go on, send them," Chris told him. "You have nothing to worry about with me unless you spill something in here."

✺

At the Hilton near Phoenix Sky Harbor Airport, FBI Special Agent Linda Monaghan and Federal Prosecutor Susan Boone are seated in a tan leather booth in the hotel restaurant. Breakfast meetings like this one, between law enforcement and the Justice Department, happen every day all over the country to discuss crimes of all sorts, but this morning, these two were there to discuss their brother's lives. After a server refills their water and tops off their coffee, they continue their conversation.

"Me? Married? No, I'm married to the job," Linda said as she poured Splenda into her cup. "What about you?"

"I'm divorced. I used to be a sucker for a pretty face and a good line, but I had to find out the hard way. Our Dad was in the Air Force. We buried him just a few days ago."

Linda reached across the table and placed her hand on Susan's.

"I'm so sorry for your loss, and so recently."

"Thank you. My brother Chris served in the Marines for twenty years. He did great in the service but withdrew after his wife was killed in a car accident. Now, he works offshore on oil rigs. Will, the youngest, never served. He's autistic." Linda felt her phone vibrate but ignored it.

"That's so sad, Chris' wife, I mean. From what you've told me, Will seems to be a good guy who got tied up with the wrong people. It happens all the time, and we both see that every day at work, don't we?" Susan nodded, withdrew her hand, and sipped at her coffee.

"Our dad died years ago," Linda continued. "But he was so proud of us." Susan had taken a moment to survey the restaurant but refocused on Linda when she heard the pause.

"Pat in the Air Force and me with the FBI. *Our* little brother Robbie was in the Army. He was stationed in Germany and was killed in a car crash on the Autobahn."

Susan reached back across to Linda and grasped her hand tight.

"Robbie was around Will's age when he died," Linda continued but then stared into space.

"I am so sorry. I feel like such as jackass sitting here. You lost your brother, and I'm here trying to save mine after he helped steal a B-17."

The two locked eyes. Their parents and one of their brothers were gone, and not one or two, but all three remaining ones were now in harm's way. The women were married to their professions and devoted to their brothers, and it was time to get to work to save them.

"So, does Will deserve to go to jail for what he's done? Maybe. Can I let that happen? Sure can't," Susan stated emphatically. Susan sat quietly and watched as Linda studied her.

"So you're going to try for immunity in exchange for Will's testimony in court."

"Absolutely," Susan stated.

"Okay. If his story checks out, I can make that happen on my side, but he has to tell us where they took her." Susan let out a breath and then got up from the table. She waved to the server for the check and then looked at Linda.

"So we have a deal?"

"We do," Linda said, nodding.

"Good. Because Will's upstairs and ready to talk."

CHAPTER FOURTEEN

As THEY ARRIVED at room 243 on the second floor, Susan knocked twice and swiped the keycard. She called out as she led Linda Monahan, her newest acquaintance in law enforcement, inside.

"Will, just me and with someone who wants to help."

Stepping into the suite, she saw Will seated at the desk just as she had left him, playing a game on her laptop. She saw him tense and began to reassure him until Linda stepped past her, taking a seat on the window sill instead of a seat at the table.

"Hi Will, it's a pleasure to meet you."

"Will, this is Linda Monaghan. Her brother was the pilot of the B-17 Mark Childress hijacked. She's here to help, so I need you to tell her everything you told me."

Susan was nervous but did her best to keep that hidden. Her brother was now in front of the FBI and needed to perform to the best of his ability. He needed to be himself, and he needed to tell the truth. Then, suddenly, Will got up from the table and extended his hand.

"Very pleased to meet you, Special Agent Monaghan.

I am very sorry any of this ever happened. I want you to know that I didn't hurt anybody. Liz and I flew out here to Phoenix to meet Miss Fleming to see about her father's wish, and when Liz said we could make that happen, I rode back out here with Mark and Liz from Texas. Then I went with Liz from Havasu to the hangar where they brought the airplane for the Make-A-Wish."

Linda shook his hand and listened attentively as she gestured for Will to take a seat.

"Good. And when the plane landed at the hangar, what did you do?"

"We sat in the BMW behind the hangar-like we were supposed to. We saw the plane land and then taxi inside. After a few minutes, Mark and the other pilots came out of the hangar. They were all happy, so it must have gone well. They got into the Suburban. Liz drove from Havasu to the hangar. I had followed her there in Mark's BMW."

Linda got up and walked to the window.

"Susan said you live out here. I can't imagine living somewhere with palm trees everywhere. It's really neat," Will said. Linda turned and laughed.

"You should be here in July." She turned, sat at the window, glanced at Susan, leaning against a bureau, and focused back on Will. "And then what happened?"

Distracted by something on the laptop, Will closed it.

"Mark drove the pilots back to the airport in Havasu so they could all fly home, and Liz and I went back to the hotel to wait for Mark. The next morning, we drove back to Texas."

"Did anyone have a gun?" she asked, watching Will for any signs of a lie.

"No. Why would they? All we were doing was helping make someone's wish."

Linda nodded slightly as she let out a breath.

"Tell me about that. The wish." Linda watched Will come alive.

"Sure. Liz found Miss Fleming on the internet. Liz said her grandfather was dying and had one wish she wanted to make happen. She said her grandfather had been in the service during World War II. He was like twenty years old and was a tail gunner in a B-17. He was supposed to fly out on a mission from England to bomb Hamburg, Germany, but he had appendicitis and had to be operated on. He couldn't go, and the plane was shot down. Everyone aboard, all of his buddies, were killed." Linda got up and stared at Susan.

"You've got to be kidding me?"

"Nope," Susan said. "I can't wait to find this Miss Fleming."

Then Linda looked at Will.

"Hey, this is a big help. I want you to know you're doing great."

Linda looked at Susan, who was beaming. She could see the pride and love for her little brother standing tall in front of a stranger from the FBI today.

"Do you want a soda? There's Diet Cokes in the little fridge."

Linda smiled and shook her head no as she returned to the bed and retook her seat.

"No, but I might need something a little stronger tonight. Thank you, though."

"You're welcome."

"Now tell her the rest of the story, Will," Susan suggested.

"So all of his life, Miss Fleming's grandfather was depressed about not being with his buddies. She said he always felt he should have died with them. She said his dying wish was to take his last breath on a B17, just like his buddies."

"So her idea was to have you hijack the plane and bring it to a hangar where? What was supposed to happen next?" Hearing that, Will became animated and stared at Susan with concern.

Suddenly, a knock at the door made them all tense. Susan looked at Linda, and they both laughed. They'd met witnesses in hotel rooms for interrogations and negotiations, but this was different. They weren't hiding anyone someone might want to silence.

"Expecting anyone," Linda whispered as she drew back her tan suit jacket and placed her hand on her weapon.

"Hey, Chris has the same," Will began.

Both women spun toward him.

"Shhh," they both whispered.

Then, the door opened.

"Housekeeping," a Hispanic woman in her mid-thirties, a hotel employee there to clean the room, said as she peeked her head in as Susan walked toward the door.

"No, we're okay. We'll be checking out soon. Thank you."

Susan threw the bolt on the door and returned, a look of relief across her face.

"Wait, Linda. We didn't hijack it. Everyone donated their time to grant his wish. Once the airplane arrived at the hangar, her grandfather would be placed on board. She said he only had days to live. Once he died, she would call Liz, and we'd go back to the hangar, and the pilots would fly the airplane home."

"Unbelievable," Linda said sternly.

"I'm telling the truth," Will protested.

"No, no, Will, not you," she assured him. "Don't you watch the news?"

Susan interrupted them.

"He doesn't like-" but Linda raised her hand to stop her.

"Will, you don't watch the news? Do you read the newspapers?"

"No, I don't," he said, taking a defensive tone. "I don't watch the news or read about it. Too many shootings. Kids killed in house fires—car crashes. I don't watch any of it. That's how I learned about Cindy's accident. Her picture was on the TV news."

"And what do you think now?" Linda asked.

"About?"

"About Miss Fleming and her dying grandfather?"

"Well, the last time I talked to Liz, she said Miss Fleming hadn't called, so I guess he's still alive." Linda pressed him.

"But what if Fleming never calls Liz?"

Based on his expression, it appeared that the question surprised him.

"Never thought of it."

"Well, maybe you should have."

Linda walked past Susan and slid a K-cup into the Keurig coffee maker.

"You think they ever clean these?" she asked as the brewer began to hiss. Then she turned to Will.

"Now, can you tell me where the hangar is?" Will perked up and quickly opened the laptop.

"I have it on MapQuest, and I can also show you where Miss Fleming's office is. We could go see her. Come look," Will said as he waved to the women.

"Will, what can you tell me about Miss Fleming?" Linda asked as she took screenshots of the MapQuest page.

"She was nice, probably around Susan's age. Maybe a little older but younger than you," Will said as he stepped away from the desk and retrieved a soda.

"She had blonde hair pulled back. She was wearing a black business suit with a gold shirt underneath and gold heels."

"What else? Taller or shorter than me? Thinner or heavier?" Linda continued.

"Taller than you, same weight as you."

"Anything else? Any distinguishing marks like a mole or a scar or?"

"She was pretty like you."

Linda blushed as she smiled at Will's proud sister, who seemed to be holding back a laugh.

"Oh, and she had an accent. It was slight, but I've heard it in the movies before."

Susan stepped close.

"That's new. You didn't mention that before," she said as she looked at Linda.

"You didn't ask," Will said as he scrolled on the computer.

"I think it was German or maybe Austrian. One of those."

Linda and Susan both cocked their heads and then laughed about it.

"A German woman pays to have an American B-17 hijacked?" Susan asked.

"Will, I have two more questions, and then we're finished."

"Okay, shoot." Susan laughed.

" Are you telling me the truth?" Linda asked.

"Yes."

"You swear?"

Will looked at Susan, seemingly unsure. She nodded it was okay.

"I swear." Linda smiled and nodded her approval.

"Last question."

"Wait, that's three." Susan laughed again as she smiled proudly.

"Did your sister tell you how to answer my questions or tell you to hide anything from me?" Will smiled before he answered.

"No, ma'am." Linda smiled.

"Good. You did very well, Will." Then she turned to Susan.

"Listen, I have a call to make, and then I'll come back up here, and we can talk a little bit more, okay?"

"Sure thing. I'm not going anywhere."

Susan followed Linda to the door, but then Linda paused and walked back to Will.

"Will, can you tell me how the black Ford van got there," she asked.

"What van? I told you it was a white Tahoe."

Linda smiled and returned to Susan at the door.

"I thought the van they put the pilots and passengers in was white," she whispered.

As Linda walked exited the room, she turned.

"It was. I just had to throw one last test at him, and he passed."

❧

Childress got back behind the wheel after filling up the car and noticed a change in Liz's expression. They were both tired, but a big payday was near, and he didn't understand her look of concern.

"Have we really thought this through?"

Childress, who had refused to let her take a turn behind the wheel since they left Texas the night before, ignored her question.

"Hey, there's two of us here," she shouted but calmed when his glare reminded her of his temper.

"What's the problem? Whatever it is, you've had a thousand miles to talk about it, so why wait until now?" She stared at Childress and sat back in her seat. She knew he was right. She'd run through every question but didn't have the answers. Perhaps he was right, she hoped—at least this time.

"Fleming hasn't called, so theoretically, the old dude hasn't died. But there weren't any facilities there to take care of them. No RVs, nothing. You don't think they slept and ate on her jet, do you?" She watched the wheels start to turn in Childress's head.

"And what about the body? What if we got there, and

they just left him to die and flew off? What if there's no money for us and just an old rotting corpse?"

"Look, no matter what, if she's not there with the money, then we know where her office is. We'll just go there and put a gun in her face. It's that simple, okay? It's not like they could have flown that thing out of there. We had the pilots!"

Childress punched the gas pedal and sped out into the mid-morning traffic.

"We'll be there soon. Everything will be fine."

Liz looked at him long and hard as he focused on the road. *You're an idiot, so I guess that makes me one too.*

CHAPTER FIFTEEN

HEADED SOUTHBOUND ON 95 from Lake Havasu City, Chris suddenly stopped on the shoulder of the road.

"Can't hold it?" Pat joked. Chris shook his head and pointed across the highway.

"That's where the police were parked late yesterday. That must be where they found the dead pilots." Pat shook his head as he stared at the yellow police tape, now torn and hanging from a stake.

"The news said there were three bodies, and the only one they'd identified so far was a pilot with a criminal record." He sat quietly for a moment and then continued.

"That jackass that stole my plane must have taken out the three who helped him."

Chris looked at Pat.

"I hope you know how lucky you are. He could have killed all of you." Pat nodded and then gestured for Chris to get going.

Twenty minutes later, Chris turned left off the highway onto a dirt road that, to Pat, looked like it was a road to nowhere.

As the bumps in the road soon increased, Pat held out as long as he could but finally requested they make a pit stop. Standing beside the pickup, Pat got rid of his coffee while on the other side, Chris stretched and then filled his travel mug from a plaid-colored Stanley thermos that looked to have seen better days. Then, just as Pat zipped up, his phone began vibrating in his jeans pocket. At first, he ignored it but thought again and checked the caller ID.

"Wondered when I'd hear from you again," Pat said, happy to hear his sister's voice.

"You'll never guess where I'm standing." As they began to talk, he looked across the back of the pickup bed to see Chris was also on the phone, and they exchanged a puzzling look. After another minute, Pat ended his call and walked around to the truck's driver's side. As Pat waited, he tapped his fingers on the top of the pickup's bed and then drummed louder until Chris laughed.

"Yeah, what are the chances? Tell Will I said hi," and ended the call. He turned to Pat.

"Did she tell you they were headed to see Diane Fleming – the one who set this whole thing up?"

Pat shook his head yes.

"But you forgot to tell me Susan is a Federal Prosecutor," Pat quipped.

Without uttering another word, Chris got back behind the wheel, started the truck, and put it in gear. Realizing he might be left to walk, Pat quickly ran to his side and jumped in. He studied Chris as they drove further down the dirt road, following it to the left, right, and back between the low, flowing hills and berms until Pat finally spoke.

"Yeah, so like you said. What are the chances you and I connect in a parking lot in Havasu while our sisters are chowing down with your brother, the unindicted coconspirator, at some hotel in Phoenix?" Suddenly, the truck slid to a halt. Chris slammed the shifter into Park and glared at his passenger.

◆

"Look," Chris said as he leaned over toward Pat. "He's a good, innocent kid with a slight disability." He watched his passenger's expression and was ready to leave him in the desert if what he uttered next didn't suit Chris. Then, he read the man's eyes and knew he'd overreacted.

"Chris, I understand what you're saying. But remember, I had a gun in my face. Hell, the prick knocked my shades off with the barrel at one point. Our sisters have cut a deal; he'll testify against the guy and his girlfriend, and they're recording his testimony now, so they have it. To anyone who sees it, they'll know he was duped into something heinous, and now he's making it right, okay?" Without answering, Chris slid the truck into Drive, and as it began to roll forward, he relaxed and smiled at Pat.

"What?" Pat asked. Chris looked through the windshield and said, "There it is, right where Will said it was." He turned and watched Pat sit up in his seat with excitement as the camo Quonset hut hangar came into view, so much so that Chris thought for a moment the man might jump out and run to it. He gave the truck some gas, followed the road along the left side of the hangar, and pointed to the rear pedestrian door as they stopped.

"That's where Will and Liz waited when the hijackers flew her in."

"He said Childress and three other men, men he'd never seen before, got into an SUV, a white Tahoe Childress had rented under an alias at the Havasu airport. Childress drove them back to the airport, returned the Tahoe, and took an Uber back to the hotel where Liz and Will were waiting." Pat sat quietly and continued to listen as he drank a bottle of water.

"Why didn't the girl and your brother follow them to the airport or let the three drive the Tahoe there directly and return it? Wouldn't that have made more sense?"

Chris shook his head and took his foot off the brake, letting the pickup crawl further along the side of the hangar.

"That makes perfect sense, but Childress said they wanted to go to a strip club first, and he knew Liz and Will wouldn't have liked it there." Pat laughed and surveyed the area.

"What a thoughtful guy that Childress," said sarcastically. "I just hope I get to tell him that face to face someday, but this time, with me holding all the cards."

Chris pulled the truck around to the front of the hangar and stopped near the slit in the doors.

"Come on, it's empty, but you should see it," Chris said as he climbed out and grabbed a flashlight from under the seat. Pat followed him through the two-foot opening between the huge hangar doors. Then, they froze as the sound of a rattlesnake's pulsating tail broke the silence.

"Shit," Chris uttered as he began to pan the floor with

the light and slowly reached for the sidearm on his thigh. "Damn it! It's in the truck."

"Marines," Pat said as he shook his head. "It's just a snake. Maybe you can just stand there until the Highway Patrol gets here. Linda said they were on the way."

Then, Chris found it with his light, and the two stepped further away from the door and watched with relief as the four-foot diamondback slithered out through the hangar doorway.

"I didn't touch anything when I was here yesterday," Chris said as he shook off the nerves the snake had caused. "But, I did kick a drum or two. They're empty, just like I told you."

Chris panned the inside with his light, walked to the opening, and peeked out.

"Come on, it's gone," he assured Pat, who followed him outside.

"Now, where'd they take her from here?" Pat said as he removed his NASCAR hat and scratched the side of his head.

"Twenty drums of fuel. That's a thousand gallons," Chris said. Pat replaced his hat, walked twenty feet from Chris, turned, and stared back at the hangar, shaking his head.

"At two hundred gallons per hour, at cruising speed, that could take her 700 miles, but that's in addition to what was on her when they landed." Chris walked to him.

"Damn, they were good. I didn't see any prints on the drums," he said. Pat nodded.

"It seems Will is the only loose end they have left now. I'm glad he's got protection now. Linda already has four agents with them at the hotel protecting Will and your sister."

The two men stood quietly, studying the terrain, the windblown runway, and some sort of bird with a wide wingspan as it flew circles high above them. Then Chris saw Pat's shoulders deflate as he walked toward the pickup.

"Hey," Chris called out. Pat turned.

"What do you say we get out of here and go find your plane?"

He was pleased as he watched Pat's posture perk up.

"Sounds like a plan," Pat called out as he climbed into the truck. Chris slid the flashlight back under his seat and opened the rear side door. He stared at all the gear he'd brought with him and shook his head when he saw his thigh holster and pistol. He thought about strapping it to this leg but shook his head no. *That bird could be anywhere by now, so I won't need that.*

He climbed in behind the wheel, started the truck, and drove back toward the highway, but then, just as they passed the hangar, Chris saw a vehicle racing toward them, a trail of dirt and silt kicked up in its wake. Then he recognized the driver. It was Childress coming straight at them.

Chris punched the accelerator, blew past the black BMW, and watched in his mirror as the car spun around and began chasing him.

CHAPTER SIXTEEN

"Who the hell's that?" Pat shouted as he buckled up and turned to watch as the car closed in fast, nearly lost in the dirt being kicked up.

"They're the ones who stole the plane," he said.

"So what are you doing?" Pat shouted. "Marines don't run!"

Chris smiled as he let off the gas and hit the brakes. Then, as the Childress hit his brakes, Chris threw the truck into 4WD, selected reverse, and punched the gas. When the two collided, the nose of the BMW slid under the pickup's high rear bumper and came to a stop. Then, Chris' training and anger kicked in. In one fluid motion, Chris removed his .45 from the center console, opened the door, and got out. There, he saw Childress' arm extend out of the BMW driver's side window, holding a gun. Without flinching, Chris threw three rounds at the driver through the windshield and took a knee as he watched Childress' gun drop to the ground. On the other side of the pickup, Pat jumped out and ran to the front of the truck for cover. Unsure where Liz was, Chris quickly reached inside the back door, grabbed his thigh holster, and stayed low as he backed up to meet Pat at the front bumper.

"You good?" Chris asked.

"So far." Chris handed Pat his .45 and then slid a black 9mm from the tan holster.

"Remember how to use one of those?"

"Sure do," Pat said.

"Any good?" Chris asked.

"A little rusty like the rest of me, but I can shoot," Pat said as they both took a knee; the seventy-year-old was a bit slower than Chris and looked under the truck. With no sign of anyone moving outside of the BMW, Chris shared his plan.

"Watch me. When I reach the driver's side, tell her to get out of the car with her hands up," Chris said. "I'll sneak around and come up behind her, so if you have to shoot, shoot low."

"What happens if she doesn't get out?" Pat asked.

"She's not stupid," Chris answered as he surveyed the area around them. "But if she is, she'll be with that prick in hell soon."

Chris checked his weapon, moving the slide to see a round in the chamber just like he left it, and began a low crawl along the driver's side of the two vehicles. As he got to Childress' window, he listened for Liz but heard nothing.

"Hey, in the passenger's side, get out of the vehicle with your hands up," Chris heard Pat shout from the safety of the front of the truck. He saw Childress' gun, threw it into the brush, and continued. Then, behind the BMW, Chris peered under the car. He saw Pat move to the right front of the pickup and heard the passenger side door of the BMW creak open slowly. He saw a bare right foot touch the ground and then a second. He continued his movement, and when he turned the corner, he saw Liz Tyler standing facing Pat, her long dark hair pulled back in a tie and her hands at her sides. Chris moved slowly and could see Pat pointing the gun as he approached her.

Suddenly, Chris yells, "Hey!" Liz spins around and swings at Chris, but he quickly leans back to avoid her left hook and drops her to the ground with a lightning-fast left jab. Then, he stands over her as she shakes her head. He moved to holster his weapon but quickly remembered he'd tossed the holster and instead slid the gun into his waist belt and stared at her.

"That's for Will."

Chris walks past Pat and studies the damage to his truck. Suddenly, Chris hears movement behind him and sees Liz holding a knife and slashing at Pat's hand holding the gun. Pat dropped the gun and stepped away, grabbing his bloody wound. Chris charged toward them. Liz reached for the gun, but Pat kicked it under the BMW.

Liz pauses for a moment. She looks at Chris, who has his gun trained straight at her eyes. She looks inside the BMW, perhaps at Childress, and then runs up a slight incline into the desert.

Chris looks at Pat's hand and then at the ground.

"Damn it," Chris says, frustrated there might be a chase. "Does she still have the knife?" Pat studied the ground as he grimaced in pain.

"I'm not sure, but that's okay; the Highway Patrol should be here soon. They'll get her."

"Screw that," Chris uttered in a low tone as he removed a gear bag from his truck and placed it on the hood of the BMW.

"Come here," he tells Pat, who follows instructions and watches as Chris rifles through the gear bag and then applies a tourniquet to Pat's hand.

"Can you work your phone?" Chris asked as he returned to the side door of his pickup and reached inside. He stepped back, holding the .30-06 hunting rifle his parents gave him for his fifteenth birthday a quarter of a century ago, and looked up the hill toward Liz.

"Seriously?" Pat called out as he watched in apparent disbelief. Chris looked at him, grinned, and switched out the weapon for a much smaller caliber. He took the .22, a Marlin bolt-action Leo had given him for his tenth birthday, raised it, and quickly found her in his scope. He thumbed off the safety.

"Call your sister. Give her an update. Describe what we're wearing so the troopers don't shoot us." Then, using the scope, Chris watched Liz run further up the incline and desert brush. He focused the crosshairs on her head and let out a breath. Slowly, he moved them lower to the outside of her right calf and pulled the trigger just as she disappeared over the top.

༄

Pat had been running on adrenaline, but after he'd been slashed the length of his thumb and Chris had stopped the bleeding, he'd begun to feel the pain. What was happening was all new to him. He'd been a pilot all his life, and although he had seen action in the Air Force, the violence he'd dealt had always been from altitude. The day Childress had shoved that gun in his face was the first time he'd been on the receiving end of one of those, and now he'd been involved in a shoot-out in the Arizona desert, his hand was severely cut, and he'd just watched someone shoot a woman with a rifle. To make matters worse, his call to Linda hadn't gone through; there was no cell service. He walked to Chris.

"How's the hand?" Chris asked. "You want some pain meds? I think I have Tylenol with codeine somewhere in there. It might be old, but -"

"Was *that* necessary?" Pat asked.

"I didn't think we could catch her," Chris quipped. "But don't worry; I just nicked her leg to slow her down."

"Boy, I wouldn't want to piss you off," Pat said as he leaned against the truck.

"You should see me without coffee, and don't scratch the paint." Pat gave Chris a curious look as he motioned with his head at the damage and the BMW wedged under it. He watched as Chris dug through a gear bag and handed him a second tourniquet.

"She might need that," Chris said. "Can you go get her? I've got a few things to do here."

Pat shook his head no as he stared at Chris.

"She's bleeding somewhere up there," Chris said, but Pat still didn't budge.

"Come on Air Force, you're not *that* old."

Pat shook his head and began walking in Liz's direction but turned and walked to the BMW. He got down on one knee and looked under the car. The .45 he'd kicked there was in reach, and he stood up, holding it with his good hand. He walked to Chris.

"Swap with me; this one's got to have some dirt in it," Pat said. Chris smiled and obliged.

"So what are you going to do while I'm hill climbing?"

"Checking to see if there's anything on him we can use before the police get here. Remember, we agreed on the way here that if we could find your bird on our own, we would. It'll remove the tarnish some people think you have on your impeccable reputation, and I just have to do it. I have to for me and my family." Pat nodded in agreement.

"That is unless you want to check the dead guy's bloody pockets?"

Pat shook his head no and began his trek up the hill. Thirty yards up, he turned to see Chris open the trunk of the BMW, pull luggage or something like it, and drop it in the dirt. Then, he refocused on the wounded animal he was tracking. As he crested the hill, he finally saw Liz lying face down about twenty yards away. He looked up at the sky and saw that same bird still circling. He took a minute to catch his breath in the heat and approached her after all the excitement down below. He called out.

"Hey, lady. Do you have any weapons on you? Roll over so I can see your hands!" She didn't respond, so he walked closer and stopped a few feet from her legs. He saw the wound, and Chris was right; he'd just nicked her enough to slow her down.

Pat kicked at her western boot, but she didn't respond. Then, he began to study her more closely.

Her arms were extended in front of her, and her hands were empty as if she had tried to block her fall. He kicked her boot again, but still, no response. He tucked the gun into his blue jeans, reached down with his good hand, his right one, and began to roll her. Then he saw it. He heard it loud and clear. She'd had a date with a rattlesnake, a large one, and lost. He wasn't sure, but it looked like she was struck, fell, and struck again. Then he saw the blood. She'd hit her head on a rock. He felt for her for a moment but then remembered everything Chris had told him as the pain in the hand she slashed throbbed.

"They say Karma's a bitch, and I guess I'll just leave it at that," Pat said in a solemn tone and then made the sign of the cross.

"Rest in the peace you didn't find here, young lady."

Pat hadn't lost sight of the snake. He'd seen plenty of them before in hikes across the southwest.

"And you better get out of here before he takes a shot at you too."

As Pat reached the hill crest, he saw Chris standing by the vehicles and raising his hands, seeming to ask, "What's up?" Pat raised his right hand, gave the OK sign, and began walking downhill. But then, something caught his eye. He squinted for a moment, rubbed them, and then squinted again. His eyes teared up, and then he continued his descent.

He took his time and switched his focus from Chris at the BMW to what had caught his eye off in the distance and back to Chris. As he neared the car at ground level, he lost sight of the anomaly in the desert and stopped. Chris had dumped one of the large gray suitcases onto the ground, scattering white bricks of cocaine. Then, as

Pat approached, Chris pointed to a black duffle he had opened in the trunk. Inside were a host of weapons, primarily high-capacity assault rifles and at least a dozen assorted handguns. Pat shook his head and walked around to the driver's side. There, he saw what was left of Mark Childress, drug and weapons trader turned hijacker and murderer, lying dead on the ground. Pat stood over him and attempted to offer some sentiment as he had on the hill over Liz, but he couldn't. This was nothing more than an animal Chris had put down.

"So where is she?" Chris asked. "There's no way she got away." Pat shook his head in agreement.

"Looks like you took out two snakes in one day, but a rattler and a rock up there finished the job." Pat studied Chris, perhaps expecting a smart remark, and was somewhat surprised by his silence.

"While you were gone, I walked back toward the hangar and got a signal. There should be some troopers and an ambulance here any time now." Then, as if they'd been staged to arrive on cue, an Arizona Highway Patrol helicopter did a quick flyover and set down at the far end of the runway as two silver and black SUVs sped down the dirt road toward them. Soon, after seeing the drugs and weapons that had been found, two of the troopers congratulated the men while another walked up the hill to find Liz, and the rest peered inside the hangar.

"Hey, where's the plane?" one called out. Chris shrugged his shoulders, but Pat looked past them at the terrain. Then, Pat's phone rang.

Linda told him she had notified the AHP while she drove with Susan to Diane Fleming's office in Phoenix and called her brother to make sure the cavalry had arrived and the two were safe.

"We're fine," Pat assured his sister but left out the part about how many stitches his hand would need. After putting their phones on speaker, the brothers told their tale and asked their sisters about Fleming.

"She's gone, long gone," Susan said.

"Yeah, the office space Liz and Will went to is empty. The building manager said she paid for one month in advance, moved in some furniture, and disappeared without leaving any forwarding info," Linda told them.

"She paid in cash," Susan added. "But you know, it just occurred to me. Do we know who owns the B-17? I know Pat was flying it during a Warbird event, but who owns it? A museum or?" While they were talking, one of the chopper's crew directed Pat toward the helicopter.

"We'll get you to the hospital in no time," the trooper said.

"Wait! What?" both women called out on the speaker. "Who needs a hospital?"

Pat shook his head in disbelief and glared at the trooper as Chris laughed.

"One of the troopers. We're fine," Chris said. Pat looked at Chris with surprise.

"Hey, listen, we'll call you in a little while," Chris said as he tapped the phone to end the call. Pat looked at his hand and told the trooper he wasn't riding in any helicopters.

"I rode here with him and intend to leave that way. Now, unless you need us for anything else, I want to show my friend here something."

The trooper nodded and continued toward the helicopter as Pat stopped and smiled at Chris.

❧

Seated at their desks in the detective division of the Palm Springs Police Department, Jones read through files and tapped his computer keyboards, taking occasional sips of cold coffee as he worked. Simms finished a bottle of peach-flavored iced tea, thanked someone on the phone, and ended a call.

"Now that was interesting," she said across the metal desks that faced each other.

"Not unless you tell me," Jones asked without looking up.

"That was a detective from the Lake Havasu City police. He was just at a nursing home interviewing a ninety-nine-year-old resident who claims he was kidnapped last week."

At first, Jones seemed to ignore what Simms had said, but finally, he looked up.

"Okay, I'm on the edge of my seat. Please continue."

Simms faked a smile and shared the rest of what the detective had shared.

"So anyway. The resident said two people posed at relatives and took him for a ride last week. He said he got confused and upset and told them he wanted to go home. He then said they took him to an airplane hangar in the desert. He said a big, dull, dark green airplane taxied into the hangar like the ones back in the war. They had him sit in a wheelchair until after some people got out of the plane. Then they drove him back to the nursing home, wheeled him to the front door, and left."

Jones got up from his chair and gave Simms a high five where she sat.

"Can he show them where the hangar was?"

"Probably not. The detective said he can't remember his name half the time."

Jones took a seat on the edge of Simms's desk. She began to reach for her gun.

"How many times have I told you." Jones raised his hands and returned to his desk.

"So why the hell would someone borrow an old man and have him sit in a hangar until a stolen airplane rolled in?"

"Got me. Did they report it to AHP?"

Simms nodded, and then the two sat quietly, thinking. Jones took a sip of his old coffee and nearly choked on it as he swallowed.

"Do they know if the old guy served in the military?"

Simms shook her head no.

"He was an optometrist from Philly. No military service," Simms answered.

"Weird, huh?" Jones stated and then tossed his 7-11 coffee container in the trash.

The two sat forward in their chairs and got back to work but were soon interrupted by a young patrolman who stuck his head in their office door.

"Did you guys see the news?" he asked, beaming.

"What?" Jones asked.

"They found the hangar where they took the B-17!"

Simms stood up and clicked the TV remote.

"Did they find the plane," she asked and dropped back into her seat when the patrolman shook his head no.

CHAPTER SEVENTEEN

CHRIS WATCHED PAT walk across the front of the camo hangar doors, then looked back at him and waved.

"Come on. Walk with me," Pat said softly. Chris nodded and caught up to Pat, and then the two followed the asphalt of the runway until it seemed to end as the desert under their feet grew denser. They walked another twenty yards, and Chris studied Pat as they kept going.

"Where are you taking me, Pat?" Chris asked. "Looking for more snakes?"

Suddenly, Pat stopped, and once Chris realized he had, he turned and walked back to him. Chris looked past him and saw the troopers focused on the bodies and the contents of the BMW and showed no interest in either of them. A Mojave County Coroner's Office tan van and at least two more unmarked vehicles had arrived.

"Pat?" Chris asked again. "You okay?"

He watched as Pat smiled and pointed further in the direction they had been walking.

"No snakes, Chris. I'm looking for a lost bird."

Chris raised his hand to block the sun and surveyed the area.

"Okay, tell me more."

"Kick at the ground, Chris, tap it with your heel."

Chris did, and to his surprise, he felt the road.

"This runway's a lot longer than I thought."

"Now, humor me, and let's keep walking." They did, walking side by side.

"When I was up on that hill, I saw something. You said the people that took her were smart, but maybe that Fleming woman was even smarter."

"How so?" Chris asked.

"Look there," Pat pointed as he kept walking. Chris stared for a moment, and then he saw it. He could see something wasn't right another fifty yards or so from where they were.

Is that desert camo? He asked himself and then began running toward it. Chris looked back at Pat, who was trying to keep up. Finally, he stopped in his tracks and stared. From a distance, this, whatever this was, blended in with the terrain, but now, up close, it was clearly a massive piece of desert camouflage, and as it got to within five feet of it, he stopped and turned, waiting for Pat.

"You see it now, Marine?" Pat asked, gushing with joy.

"I sure as hell do, Pat. I think you found her."

Pat placed his good hand on Chris' shoulder and corrected him as he panted from the run.

"No, *we* found her."

Chris kicked at the ground, and Pat soon joined in. After a few minutes, Chris found the edge of the covering and tried to lift it somehow. Too big and too heavy, he thought about shouting for the troopers to help but then changed his mind and pulled a large switchblade out of his pocket. He opened the blade and held it out for Pat.

"You do it," Chris insisted, but Pat shook his head as he held up his injured hand.

"Cut the damn thing before I stroke out from all the excitement!"

Chris smiled and went to cutting. He opened a slit in the covering and continued cutting until there was a six-by-four-foot opening. He closed the knife and slid it into his pocket.

"Age before beauty, Air Force. Now get in there."

Pat paused at the opening and then stepped inside. Chris looked back toward the troopers and saw that someone must have noticed what they were doing as three vehicles were now speeding toward them. He smiled and then followed Pat.

Inside, he stopped beside Pat and looked at the large shadows they were casting on the national treasure they had just found. The big, beautiful B-17 rested underneath the cover that seemed big enough to cover a ball field, and as the troopers stepped inside and lit the area with their flashlights, it became clear just how smart Fleming had been.

"Look, they dug into the hillside and then backed her in," one trooper called out as another pointed out the aluminum framework erected to cover the plane and simulate a sloping hillside. Then, Chris realized Pat had stepped outside and joined him.

"Pat, you okay?' Chris asked as other troopers began to arrive.

"I never thought I'd see her again," he said in a hushed tone, his emotions beginning to take over.

"Do you want to go inside, check out the cockpit, make sure they didn't hurt her?"

Pat didn't answer. He looked at Chris, patted him on the chest, a tear in his eye, and began walking back toward the pickup. Chris waited for a time, opting to give Pat some space, but broke out into a jog and caught up to him as he neared the tangled vehicles.

"Hey Pat, wait up," Chris called out, but Pat kept walking. Frustrated, he jumped in front of the tired pilot.

"Wait. What the girls said got me thinking. Childress stole the plane and delivered it to Fleming after they let all of you go. Then she hid it and left. That makes no sense. It's worth millions, isn't it?" Pat walked around Chris but stopped and turned to him.

"I'd say they're priceless, but that's just me. You're right, though; this doesn't make sense. Someone put a lot of time, effort, and money to hide her here like that. It can't be an insurance scam. They took too good care of her to claim it lost and then bring her back."

Chris saw Pat was now lost in thought but grabbed him by the arm and began walking toward the truck.

"So if this isn't an insurance scam, what the hell is this," Chris asked.

"I think our little sisters are already on that," Pat answered and heard Chris laugh.

"Little sisters? I don't know about yours, but Susan's a wildcat. Never corner her and never screw with the family." Now it was Pat's turn to chuckle.

"Oh, if you ever meet Linda, you'll be impressed. It sounds like they might be cut from the same mold."

As they arrived at his pickup, Chris reached into the truck's back seat and removed a small cooler. He handed Pat an orange Powerade, stood back, and surveyed the damage to his pickup while downing a water bottle. Then, without flinching, he got behind the wheel of his Toyota and drove it off the front of the BMW as two men dressed in forensic uniforms shouted and waved for him to stop. He ignored them until a trooper raised his hand and placed the other on the weapon on his hip holster.

"What the hell's the matter with you," the trooper shouted as he approached the driver's window.

"Fuel tank wasn't leaking, so no need to tow it, right?" The trooper stared at Chris and then looked across at Pat, who just shrugged his shoulders and smiled.

"Must be a Marine thing, I guess," Pat called out.

The trooper told Chris to get out of the truck and hand him the keys, which Chris did.

"Let me make sure they don't need this for anything, and then, and only then, you'll get the keys back."

"Okie dokie," Chris said and then dropped the tailgate and took a seat. Pat walked over and sat beside him.

"So where were you going, anyway?" Pat asked.

"Lunch. I'm starving."

"You know, I'm not sure I know who owns that B-17. I've flown it and a lot like her, but I always assumed the museum or the air show people owned them. Some wealthy people own them. They get willed to museums or lent to them, and some non-profits own them, but I just don't recall for her. What's missing? What are you getting at?"

Chris turned and stared at Pat.

"Motive."

᧞

The men sat quietly and watched the forensics team work until Pat's phone rang. He hopped off the tailgate and answered it as he walked toward the hillside.

"Is it true, Pat? Did they find her?"

It was the president of the air museum calling, and Pat shared the news, related how they spotted her and that she appeared to be in good shape.

"Well, I'm headed there now, and I want you to oversee her inspection before we get her home. Can you do that for me? You know her better than anyone."

Pat was torn. He'd felt like a loser for surrendering the plane without a fight; he'd been the target of jokes on late-night TV shows, death threats and abuse on social media, and been threatened in parking lots when recognized as the guy and been called names that cut him to the core. But he loved that airplane, and if the last thing he did was make sure she was fit and ready for others to fly, he'd do it and then find something else to keep him busy. *Maybe it's time for me to learn how to play golf, damn it.*

᧞

CHAPTER EIGHTEEN

WHEN IT COMES to aviation or law enforcement, it pays
to have friends, and Linda Monahan didn't hesitate to
ask when she needed a big favor. Rather than drive the
four hours west from Phoenix, she took a very short
flight aboard a small private jet. She was soon standing
at the front door of the contemporary ranch-style home
of thirty-eight-year-old hedge-fund aficionado William
Fleming. As she swung the silver knocker again, she looked
past the Federal Prosecutor from the Western District of
Texas and the young Will Boone. She nodded at the two
young FBI Special Agents who had met them at the plane
and were ordered by their field office boss, a classmate of
Linda's long ago at Quantico, to provide security and assist
as needed. Minutes later, Fleming led them through the
house into his office. Linda and Susan followed his lead
and sat facing his clear, see-through desk. Will hung back
and studied a variety of warbird photos mounted on the
only opaque wall in the room. The rest were glass, floor
to ceiling.

Fleming lit a cigar and plopped down in a low-back tan leather chair.

"Okay, I'm intrigued. Tell me more," he suggested, and then Susan turned to Will and waved for him to join them. Without another chair, Will leaned against the glass wall. Fleming cringed as he saw Will put his hands behind him on the glass.

"Like Linda told you on the plane, Liz introduced me as her little brother and suggested I play with the dogs people had in the park, so I did. Later, I saw them come out of the office, and Liz waved to me, so I approached them. Miss Fleming shook my hand. She said I was doing something extraordinary for a veteran and her family and that she would never forget it or me. Then I saw her at the hangar in Arizona, and I wanted to say hi to your grandfather and thank him for his service, but she wouldn't let me. He seemed upset and confused, so I didn't push it."

"Wow," Fleming said as he dumped the cigar in an ashtray and moved a chair from the far side of his office for Will to use. As he retook his seat behind the desk, Susan had a question.

"When did you last see your sister, Mr. Fleming?"

"Oh, it's been a while. Maybe a year. But I never imagined she was capable of doing anything like this." Will fidgeted in his seat, and Susan laughed as it creaked.

"So it's really that simple. Envy and revenge. As I told you on the phone, she was furious, absolutely livid, when our grandfather's will was read. In truth, I think she went batshit crazy. My sister loved that plane. I think she lost her virginity in it, for Christ's sake. She also flew away in it with one of her many husbands right after their wedding.

A knock at the door was heard, and then a Hispanic woman in her early sixties, Linda thought, wearing a black maid's uniform, pushed a cart carrying a tray of coffee, water, and sodas toward his guests.

"Thank you, Rita," Fleming said and then gestured dismissively for her to leave.

Linda looked at Susan and smiled inside as their expressions matched. *Asshole.*

"Thanks, Rita," Will called out as he cracked the seal on a Diet Coke. The woman nodded and a slight smile as she walked out of the room. Then, the focus returned to Diane.

"Our condolences on the loss of your grandfather, Mr. Fleming," Susan said, the pain of her family's loss still fresh in her heart and mind.

"Thank you."

"So tell us about his Will and how you got the plane, and she didn't," Linda said as she sat forward in her seat. "We accessed the documents, but I'd like to hear what fueled that decision." Fleming nodded and then got up and walked to the opaque wall. He stared at the photo of the family's cherished B-17. Susan and Linda both joined him there.

"That's Charles Fleming, my grandfather, our parents William and Monika, and me with Diane. I think we were twelve and ten at the time."

"So she's your little sister?" Fleming nodded, touched the photo, and then returned to his seat. Linda and Susan exchanged looks, curious ones, and turned toward him.

"So Charles left you the plane. Where's William and Monika in all of this?"

"Dead. They were killed in an avalanche in Switzerland a month after that picture was taken. We were supposed to be with them, but they treated it like a second honeymoon and wanted alone time together. So we stayed here in America. If we hadn't, who knows, we all might have been killed."

Linda shook her head in disbelief and watched Susan return to the photo and study it.

"So Charles raised you," she asked. Charles nodded and then relit his cigar.

"He was wealthy, our parents were wealthy, and had set up trusts for us just in case. Diane and I received millions from their estate from our sixteenth through our twenty-first birthdays. But I noticed something changed in her after their death. She grew cold. Angry. She wanted to move to Switzerland to be closer to where they had celebrated their wedding before the accident, but Charles wouldn't have it."

Suddenly, Will began to speak but let out a burp from the soda. Embarrassed, he excused himself and then had a question of his own.

"So, how did your grandfather get the B-17 in the first place?"

Linda took her focus from William and smiled as she observed Susan's look of pride.

"Good question, young man. World War II may have ended nearly eighty years ago, but there are still some people and organizations in America who have an issue with Germans, especially those who were involved in that war."

Linda looked back at the photo on the wall and then returned her attention to Fleming.

"How do you mean?" she asked.

"Because my grandfather fought for Germany during the war. He fled to South America as a seaman on a ship. There, he made his money and eventually returned to his fatherland years later after it was rebuilt. Then he moved here, as far from Germany as he could, to the west coast of America, the land of opportunity."

"That doesn't make sense. Did he fly here in it or what," Will asked. Fleming laughed.

"No, Will. He bought it for closure. His parents, our great-grandparents, were killed by a

B17 during a bombing run over Hamburg. Once he had the money to buy one in America, he did. He had it restored and may have intended to do something stupid with it, but as the years passed, his anger and the memories of the war softened, especially when he saw how much fun we had playing in it as kids. He also realized how much opportunity this country had provided him. He changed his mind and eventually loaned it to one museum and then another."

"This reads like a movie," Linda said as she sat back and processed what she had just heard.

᪗

Susan had listened intently to everything the man had said, and then the prosecutor in her needed more. She reached back, fixed a coffee, cleared her throat, and now it was her turn.

"You said earlier that Diane lost her virginity in the plane. Do you know that to be a fact?" Fleming nodded.

"Okay, how do you know that?" Fleming smiled.

"Because they found her underwear in it, the night of her sixteenth birthday party, beneath the cockpit hanging off the Norden bombsight. It was sacrilegious as far as I'm concerned, and so did Charles. He had taken friends on a tour of the hangar where he kept his cars and plane collections. He was so ashamed and embarrassed that he didn't talk to her for a year." Susan shook her head and looked at Will, who was focused on a hummingbird hovering near a hanging flower plant in the desert garden.

"But he let her fly in it later?" Linda asked.

"Yes. She has a way about her. She gets what she wants," Fleming said, following Will's eyes and smiling at the bird.

"Where do you think she is now?" Susan asked.

"She has a place in Munich but won't be there. She's like a snake. She'll sliver from there to Zermatt. That's where our parents died. She has a place there, and of course, there's no extradition." Susan got up, and Linda followed her lead.

"It'll be a while before an arrest warrant is issued for her, but if you have those addresses, it will save us some time," Linda said as she placed one of her cards on Fleming's desk.

Fleming smiled and walked around his desk, stopping before Will to break his trance.

"I'll email them today. Now, unless there's anything else, let me show you out."

They followed their host to the front door and nodded at the agents near their sedans. Susan turned and shook Fleming's hand.

"One last question, Mr. Fleming. Law enforcement on the scene told me that the plane was very well protected. She wasn't just left there with a camo stadium cover pulled over her. She was taken care of. If Diane did do all of this, why not just destroy it so you could never have it?"

"You'd have to ask her if you ever find her," he answered, extending his hand to Linda Monahan. Suddenly, a white Dodge Charger sedan drove up and stopped alongside the FBI vehicles. Detective Simms held her badge wallet out the driver's window as Detective Jones jumped out of the passenger side door, red-faced, and stormed toward Linda.

"What the hell are you doing here," he nearly yelled. Susan moved her right foot back and prepared to drop the cop if he pushed anything too far. Linda didn't budge, but Will stepped to the side and looked at Fleming.

"I've seen my sister in action; this is going to be good."

"They found the plane. It appears his sister paid to have it taken. She's probably in Switzerland; if she is, she's untouchable," Linda told him.

"When were you going to call us? Ever heard of professional courtesy?" Jones asked.

"Oh, like the courtesy you extended to my brother while interrogating him?"

Fleming stepped closer. Susan relaxed her stance and just watched.

"Wait, who's your brother?" Fleming asked.

"Pat Monahan, the pilot who protected his passengers by doing what the hijackers demanded. He's the same one who, led by her brother Chris and her brother Will, found it south of Lake Havasu." Jones looked back at his partner, who had gotten out of the car and was standing with the FBI agents, watching.

"Well, congratulations, glad they found her, and have a nice day," Jones said as he returned to the sedan.

Twenty minutes later, after thanking William Fleming for his assistance, the three were back aboard their ride, flying east toward the Lake Havasu City Airport and a rendezvous with their brothers.

∾

At ten o'clock the next morning, Pat Monahan sat quietly in the pilot's seat of his beloved B-17. The huge camo coverings had been removed, the aluminum framework disassembled, and the warbird towed to the hangar just after sunrise. The bright sun was nearly blinding as the massive doors opened wide.

He scanned the gauges and controls, looking for anything indicating foul play or neglect. Suddenly, he heard footsteps approaching him as someone crossed the catwalk over the bomb bay doors. He turned to see his boss, the air museum's boss Mike Horton, coming toward him. He quickly moved to get up from the seat, but Horton waved at him to stay seated, gave him a pat on the shoulder, and sat in the co-pilot's spot.

"Stay there, Pat," Horton insisted. "So, how is she?"

"So far, so good. Believe it or not, they took care of her. I don't think anyone has found a darn thing wrong other than they snapped a mast antenna when they covered here with the tarps.

Horton nodded his approval.

"When do you think she'll be ready to go home?"

"I think the mechanics said they'd be finished tomorrow, and the FAA's already given their blessing. I've never seen so many people descend on one spot just wanting to help."

Horton smiles as he looks through the cockpit window at the men working below.

"There has to be a few thousand people a day coming here to take a look from up on the hills. Wish we could charge admission," Horton joked. Pat laughed and ran his hands along the sides of the yoke.

"The Arizona Highway Patrol's been a big help keeping them at a distance. Then there's all the damn news trucks."

"Yep. Everything from CNN and FOX to the BBC and some European broadcasters are out there, too. This little episode might have a silver lining for the appreciation and preservation of these warbirds. We have a happy story, a great news story for a change."

Horton sat quietly for a minute, then put his hand on the co-pilot's yoke cover and cleared his throat.

"So when will she be ready to go," Horton asked.

"I'd say the day after tomorrow once you get a fuel truck here. The bastards that took her were pretty clever. Those empty fuel drums were just props to make us think they flew her away. She's about out of fuel." Pat got up from the pilot's seat and stepped down, now able to stand upright below the top turret.

"Who's coming to get her," he asked as he turned away from Horton.

"What are you talking about, Pat?"

"Who's flying her home?"

"You're this plane's pilot, so I hope you are."

Horton got up from the co-pilot's seat, stepped down, and shook Pat's hand. Pat did his best but couldn't wipe the tears away fast enough and laughed when he saw Horton choked up, too.

Then, a man's voice called out from somewhere beneath them.

"Hey, stop fooling around up there. Get back to work!"

Pat and Horton burst out into laughter and did just that.

∽

A month later, at Leo Boone's family retreat on Lake LBJ near Johnson City, Texas, Linda Monaghan, Susan, and Chris Boone watch from the lakeside deck as Will Boone and Pat Monaghan push away from the dock in a small boat. Chris sips his beer as he turns down the music and props his long legs up on the cooler.

"It's funny, but Pat reminds me a lot of our dad," Chris said from behind gold mirror sunglasses.

"I've been thinking that too," Susan said, shaking her head as she smiled at Linda.

"Want to hear what Pat and I said last night?" The Boones both nodded. "It's that Will reminds us both so much of Robbie."

∽

On the lake, Will laughed as Pat attempted to bait a fishing hook as the boat rocked gently.

"You haven't spent much time on the water, have you?"

Pat continued to fidget with it and shook his head.

"Nope. Most of my time's been in the air."

"But I thought you guys landed on aircraft carriers," Will continued, and Pat shook his head again.

"No, sir. That's the Navy. Air Force always takes off and lands at a base, not a boat."

"I love flying," Will said and then laughed as he reached across, taking the hook and bait from Pat.

"Here. I'll show you one more time. After that, I'll have to charge you."

They both laughed.

"So what happens next?" Pat asked him as he leaned in close and studied Will's moves.

"Hook goes into the water, and then we catch something. All that time high up in the air getting to you?"

"So you can bait a hook and tell jokes. Feel like getting thrown in?" The two laugh again, this time so loudly that Chris shouts from the dock.

"You're scaring the fish!"

In the boat, Pat reached across and took back his freshly baited hook.

"Last night, Chris said he was heading back to the gulf soon, and Susan said her caseload was bigger than ever." Will picked up his rod and cast away.

"So I have an idea if you're interested. After Chris and Susan go back to work, you should come out to Palm Springs."

"Okay. Then what?"

"You're teaching me how to fish, so I'll teach you how to fly."

᪈

Back on the dock, Linda, Susan, and Chris turn their attention to the two on the boat and watch as Will jumps up, waving at them while Pat shakes his head, each hand holding onto a side of the boat.

"Pat must have told him," Linda said, her shades hiding her tears.

"What?" Susan asked.

"He wants Will to come to Palm Springs so he can give him flying lessons."

Susan looked at Chris, who smiled and shook his head with approval.

"It might be the best thing for him, Susan. Get himself a fresh start. Free you up to focus on work but also on you, for the first time in years," Chris told her as he opened the cooler and passed her a beer.

"He could stay with Pat first to see how it works out, and if it does, Mike Horton's already told Pat that Will can work at the air museum as a tour guide if he wants to. That place has been packed ever since you two got the B-17 back."

"They really hit it off, haven't they," Susan asked Chris.

"He's a big boy now. He can make his own decisions. But, can you let your baby brother go?" Susan gets up from her seat and walks to the edge of the dock. She stares at Will. She saw the joy in him and then his concern as he seemed to wait for her reaction. Then, she shoved both thumbs straight into the air and watched Will shout with joy as he jumped into the lake.

CHAPTER NINETEEN

WEDGED INTO A bulkhead aisle seat in economy class, as other passengers bumped him with backpacks, bags, and duty-free purchases as they passed, Chris adjusted his headphones and sunglasses and fastened his seat belt for the overnight flight to Europe.

Beside him, a frail woman, perhaps in her eighties, he thought, nudged his side.

"Are you going over for work or vacation?" she asked. As he removed his headphones and shades, he smiled at the woman he towered over, then paused as the aircraft's captain made an announcement on the PA.

"Once again, this is your pilot speaking. Flight time to Munich is just under nine hours. So sit back, relax, watch some movies, or get some sleep. We'll have you there just in time to see the sunrise." Chris cringed. He'd flown long-haul flights around the world for work more times than he cared to remember or could. But this time, things were different. Aside from his workaholic sister in San Antonio, there wasn't much there for him anymore. His father, Leo, was now at rest with his mother and late wife, while

Will was now hard at work in Palm Springs, working at the air museum and learning how to fly with an incredible mentor and newfound friend. Looking ahead, the life he'd decided on, the lonely one with few entanglements, didn't seem as appealing as it once was, and the nine hours riding in a crowded tin can made him begin to reconsider everything.

"So Munich. Is it for work or for fun," the woman asked again. Chris leaned forward and looked to the seat beside her at the elderly man asleep and free from bother.

"Is that your husband," Chris asked. He watched as she turned and placed her hand on his as he slept.

"Yes, it is. We've been married for sixty-one years. He's not been well, so we're going to Germany to visit his brother. He's not well, and this might be the last time we get to make a trip like this." Chris smiled and placed his large hand over hers.

"Congratulations," he told her. "I'm headed for work on an oil rig in the Gulf, but

I'm stopping in Munich and then Zermatt for a few days to surprise someone."

"That's nice. I'll bet it's a woman if I'm not being too forward. Will she be happy to see you?" Chris grinned, and that made the woman smile.

After a day in Munich to reset his body clock and visit the Hofbräuhaus, Chris arrived in Zermatt by train and checked into a small, cozy room on the second floor of a Bavarian chalet. After Linda Monahan provided him with Diane Fleming's passport photo and Swiss address and

cautioned him not to do anything rash, he assured her he'd behave. He spent the day surveilling the area with hopes of spotting the woman. Without any luck, he spent his first night staring at the magnificent Matterhorn, the areas with snow radiating the full moon's light. The following day, though, things were much different. Suddenly, he saw her as he sipped a steaming coffee and studied the mountain hikers, trekkers, and tourists that flooded the town daily. Her photo didn't do her justice. His brother was right; she was beautiful. He watched as he passed by and scanned for bodyguards but came up empty. He smiled. Hours later, Chris pressed his gun against Diane Fleming's temple as she lay in bed and covered her mouth with his gloved hand.

His plan was simple, and her lack of common sense left her vulnerable, and he'd learned years before to exploit those opportunities.

"I'm going to remove my hand. If you do anything other than quietly answer my questions and follow my directions, I'll have to hurt you. Understand?" She nodded, her eyes open wide and her nostrils begging for air.

Chris removed his hand but continued to hold the gun close.

"My brother sent you to kill me?" Diane asked.

"No, you could have got *my* brother killed, so I came to bring you back and face a judge." Diane's face showed confusion, then surprise as she sat up and stared at Chris.

"You're Will's brother?"

"Sure am." Chris stood up. "Now, get dressed."

"So my brother didn't send you?" she asked again. Chris shook his head no.

"You can put the gun down. I'll come with you voluntarily. It's time I went public and made a deal with the authorities. Once they hear what I have to tell them about William, I should call him Wilhelm; perhaps they will."

᷈

In an interrogation room at the Palm Spring Police Department, Detectives Jones and Simms sat across from Diane Fleming, who had sat there for an hour demanding to see an attorney and refusing to answer any of their questions.

"Okay, okay," Simms told her, but I can tell you right now, we can hold you on felony charges for your involvement in the theft of that plane, the murders of three men, and at least three conspiracy charges. Your brother told us why you stole the plane. Is he right?"

Fleming stared at the detectives and then turned to the mirror window on the wall to her left. She let out a sigh and sat back in her chair.

"I overheard my grandfather and brother a few weeks before my sixteenth birthday. They thought I was asleep, but I snuck down the stairs to see what was going on and saw them in the study; both were dressed in Nazi uniforms, watching war videos of B-17s being attacked and blown out of the sky by the German Luftwaffe. It was like some sick Halloween party. They were really enjoying it."

᷈

Watching from behind the glass, Chris and Pat stood side by side.

"I still can't believe you pulled it off, and she's sitting right in front of us."

Chris, tired from the adventure, nodded.

"You know, I really want to take her bastard brother and drop him like a bomb from the B-17. Maybe over the Hoover Dam. But we'd have to do it at night, and I only know one guy who can fly those."

"You do, do ya?" Pat answered.

"What do you think?" Chris asked. Pat cocked his head.

"You're serious?"

"As a heart attack," Chris responded. Pat stepped to the glass, stared at Diane, and then turned to face Chris.

"Her brother's going to jail, so his bomb bay door will see plenty of action, if you know what I mean." Chris laughed.

"I think you're right, Pat, and that would suit me just fine."

They refocused on Fleming as she continued to tell her story.

⋦

"When I confronted my brother the next day, he told me I could never talk about what I had seen with anyone or grandfather would ship me off to a boarding school and never be heard from again. My parents had just died, I was in a fragile state of mind, and I knew I had no place else to go. Nowhere else to turn."

"Sounds like bullshit to me," Jones said as he checked his watch and began to get up.

"Your brother said your grandfather caught you having sex in the B-17. You embarrassed the family, so he sent you away. That's why you had the plane stolen, isn't it," Jones pushed.

The men watched through the glass as Fleming became enraged.

"I never had sex in that plane. He may have, but I never did. My brother needed something to push my grandfather over the edge and send me away, so he went into my room, took my underwear, and hung it over the bombsight in the nose of the plane. When my grandfather took people at my birthday party for a tour that night, he liked to show off his possessions. He saw my under-wear and freaked out. He came and found me, and within hours, my party was over, my suitcase packed, and I was flown to Austria. I spent two years at a special school near Berchtesgaden. You know about Berchtesgaden, yes?"

"What made him think the panties were yours? They could have belonged to anyone at the party that night," Simms suggested.

"Because they had my name embroidered in them," Fleming shouted. "They had been a Christmas gift from my mother."

"And you've remained in Europe since then," Jones asked.

"For the most part, yes. My parents left me a lot of money, and once I reached eighteen, my grandfather couldn't keep me there anymore. I never spoke to either of them since that night, but when I read my grandfather's Will, I had to do something. That bastard wasn't going to get control over that plane. Deep down, my grandfather had always wanted to blow it up. That's why he acquired it in the first place because, during the war, a bomb from a flying fortress killed his parents. I knew my brother might have wanted to grant a dying wish and to spite me, so I took it. I took it to save it."

"And to say F-you to your brother," Jones stated. Fleming nodded.

"So the plane is safe now, back at the museum," Simms told her. "And you're here to face a judge. I understand why you took it, but besides an embarrassing story about your brother, there's not much here. You have no real defense or excuse for what you did. You put people's lives at risk. People died. We need something more to even consider negotiating a plea deal."

Fleming sat quietly for a time.

"What I did saved a national treasure that has to be worth something. And the ones that are dead were all criminals, so you could say *they* can't hurt anyone anymore. But I do have something on my brother you might be able to use," she said, sitting up with hope in her tired eyes.

"I may have been sent away, but I maintained contact with many of my friends here, friends from school. People with money swim in the same pools, and over the years, William got into investing and did some creative bookkeeping, they have told me. Illegal things that the SEC might be interested in."

"Bullshit," Jones said as he shook his head. "If they give your brother up, they admit their guilt."

"I call bullshit back, detective. The dumb ass emailed them proposals; he put his shady planes on paper. They all said no, but they kept the emails. That is where the SEC can look. They sent them to me. I printed them and kept them just in case I needed them. And I kept the video I took of them that night, wearing those uniforms, applauding the planes being shot down." Simms sat up, looked at the mirror, and smiled.

"Now *that's* something we can deal with. When can we get to see the evidence and the video? We can leave the SEC to do their work, but we can leak the video to shame your brother so he'll never be able to show his face in public again."

Fleming shook her head as she turned to the mirror and glared.

"They're back in Zermatt!"

Jones opened his phone and entered some notes, but Simms shook her head.

"Wait. I still have a few questions. What about the old man? Why did you drag that poor soul into the charade?" Simms waited for an answer, and when one didn't immediately come, she began tapping her nails on the metal table between them. Jones looked up.

"It's never good when she does that. You should answer her."

Simms watched, expecting to see wheels turning in Fleming's head, but instead, she saw a tear form in the corner of the woman's left eye. Then she spoke.

"I thought I needed a sentimental hook to sell it to Liz and then to Will so they felt they were helping someone, a veteran in his last days. I had no idea Will came from a military family, but it worked. I didn't meet Childress until he showed up with the plane, but from the moment he climbed out of it, I could tell he was dangerous and had the nurse immediately take the gentleman away. I'm not proud of that part of this, but I can tell you, and you can check, that the man's care has been upgraded. They're now treating him like a VIP, and he'll be as comfortable and secure as possible until the day he dies." Simms nodded, perhaps giving her approval, but then it was Jones' turn to raise a question.

"What about the people that helped you? The ones in the hangar, the ones who dug out the hillside and stowed the plane under those huge tarps?"

"All friends. It's good to have friends, ones you can bet your life on. Ones who will never let you down, never give you up, and never let on they knew anything about what happened out in the desert," Fleming told them.

◈

Behind the glass, Pat and Chris stood quietly and processed what they had just heard.

"She's right about friends, old and new," Pat whispered.

Chris put his arm on Pat's shoulder and patted it.

"She sure is," Chris said.

"Do you want to head out to the airport? Will's scheduled for a lesson this afternoon.

"Wouldn't miss it for the world," Chris answered.

◈

A week later, Jones and Simms knocked at William Fleming's front door, accompanied by four FBI agents and a K-9 unit from the Palm Springs Police. As Rita opened the door, she smiled and called out for her boss. Then, as William approached the door, a black and brown German

Shepherd barked as Jones smiled and held his index finger across his upper lip.

"Herr Fleming, we have a warrant for your arrest."

Seated across the road in a black SUV, Diane Fleming watched as the detectives placed her brother in handcuffs. She shook her head as justice was served.

"Okay, let's head to the airport."

∾

The blinding California sun and desert heat of Palm Springs was the polar opposite of where Chris Boone had found Diane Fleming in the Swiss Alps, but soon she'd be in yet another environment, behind bars. As Fleming walked to the private jet she had chartered, planning a quick stop off for a shopping spree on Fifth Avenue in New York before continuing to Switzerland, two FBI Special Agents approached her, badge wallets in hand.

"So it's over. You got him," she asked, but reading their rigid expressions, she tensed.

"So did you?" she asked.

"Linda Monaghan, I'm with the FBI," the lead agent said as she stopped right in front of her.

"You're under arrest. Turn around and put your hands behind your back," Monaghan demanded. Instead of following the command, Fleming took two steps back and looked at the jet.

"Don't even think about it," the agent stated.

"But I made a deal; I am free to go," Fleming insisted and then realized she'd been had.

"You made a deal with the Palm Springs Police

Department. They don't have the authority to negotiate all of your sins away."

Fleming's head and shoulders dropped as she let go of a beige leather Gucci tote. She turned and placed her hands behind her and tensed as she felt the handcuffs tighten around her wrists. Then, she felt the agent step closer, too close.

"You thought you could kidnap a confused old veteran, steal a national treasure, take advantage of an autistic young man, put lives at risk, and screw with my brother?" Monaghan whispered as she looked past the private jet and saw the recovered B-17 resting inside a nearby hangar.

"But," Fleming began.

"But my ass," Monaghan replied and then told Fleming her rights as she escorted her to their ride, guided her into the back seat, and fastened the belt.

∽

Linda Monaghan closed the door, looked across the tarmac toward the B-17 that was now back where she belonged, safe and sound, and then waved to her brother Pat as he, Will, and Chris walked from the shadows of the plane's wing and clapped their hands in approval.

"And justice is served," Chris said proudly.

"Are you going to hang around here all day? Don't you have a plane to catch?" Will asked as he prodded Chris in the ribs.

"Sure do, and you have another lesson," Chris said. He surveyed his surroundings and let out a sigh.

"You okay?" Pat asked. Chris thought for a moment and nodded.

"Yeah, just not looking forward to spending the next fourteen hours surrounded by snoring tourists on my flight to Athens," he told them.

"They've got oil rigs in Greece?" Pat asked.

"Guess so," Chris said.

"You could stay," Will said as he stepped close to his big brother.

Chris smiled, messed Will's hair, picked up his black duffle, and began walking toward the exit.

"I'll see ya when I see ya," Chris called out without turning. Will and Pat watched for a moment, and then Will set off running toward the trainer plane while Pat tried to keep up. As Chris passed the open hangar doors, he gazed one last time at the B-17 that he was so proud to have helped rescue. Then, a ten-year-old girl taking a tour of the air museum with her school class called out.

"Hey mister, do you know anything about this plane?" Chris smiled and walked to her. He dropped his bag and took a knee beside her.

"I sure do."

THE END

Printed in Great Britain
by Amazon

49544830R00096